First Awakenings: Project Gliese 581g Book 2

By S.E. Smith

Acknowledgments

I would like to thank my husband Steve for believing in me and being proud enough of me to give me the courage to follow my dream. I would also like to give a special thank you to my sister and best friend, Linda, who not only encouraged me to write, but who also read the manuscript. Also to my other friends who believe in me: Julie, Jackie, Christel, Sally, Jolanda, Lisa, Laurelle, and Narelle. The girls that keep me going!
—S.E. Smith

Science Fiction Romance
First Awakenings: Project Gliese Book 2

First E-Book\print Published March 2017
Cover Design by Melody Simmons

Summary: A Navy Commander on an exploratory mission into space wakes on an alien world and must accept help from the assassin sent to kill the survivors of the Gliese 581 while being thrust into an intergalactic Civil War.

ISBN (paperback) 978-1-942562-73-3
ISBN (eBook) 978-1-942562-74-0

Published in the United States by Montana Publishing.

{1. Science Fiction Romance – Fiction. 2. Space Opera – Fiction. 3. Action/Adventure – Fiction. 4. Suspense – Fiction. 5. Romance – Fiction.}

www.montanapublishinghouse.com

Synopsis

Lieutenant Commander Ashton "Ash" Haze has always embraced two things in his life: adventure and women, but when he awakens on an alien planet, there's no time for anything other than survival – or so he thinks.

Kella Ta'Qui is a Turbinta – a guild that discards their genetic identities in favor of what they train to become: assassins. Her first mission is to find and kill whatever was inside the unusual capsule that landed on Tesla Terra, but predator becomes prey when she is wounded by her target. Dazed and confused, she stumbles into a group who plan to sell her to the highest bidder – until a rescuer appears.

Can an easy-going Navy pilot and an alien assassin work together to reach the location of one of the other capsules on the cutthroat Turbintan planet, or will Ash find himself served up to the Legion for the highest number of credits? Whatever happens, the war has begun with the first awakening of the resistance – and Ash is right in the middle of it.

Table of Contents

Chapter 1

"Warning... Oxygen level is currently at two percent," a soft, feminine voice announced.

"Speak to me, baby," Ash said in a sexy murmur, his eyes closed and his mind preoccupied with an amazing dream. He was hearing his current lady love's voice while they were entwined on a beach in Hawaii.

"Commander Haze, oxygen levels are critically low. External environmental readings show atmospheric conditions suitable for human life. I hope they are, otherwise you are toast. Please prepare for capsule opening in one minute... fifty-nine seconds... fifty-eight seconds... fifty-seven seconds...."

Ashton Haze's eyes popped open. His breathing sped up, loud in the claustrophobic space. He struggled to control it. A cold, clammy sweat coated his dark mocha skin and his left temple ached. *Of course a damn good dream like that would turn into a nightmare like this. Almost worse than the words 'I do' and 'I'm pregnant'! ...Well... yeah, not quite as bad as that.*

The continuing countdown had him frantically searching both his foggy brain and the pod for some way to halt the capsule from opening. He was dead either way, because unless he had miraculously returned to Earth, there was no way the sarcastic nerd from MIT, Erin Wise's, calculations could be right. He knew everyone had to die sometime, it was just being ejected into space was not the way he would have chosen to go.

"Shit! I'll take 'I do' or 'I'm… preg…' – aw hell, just give me a way to stop the top from opening, Erin," Ash muttered, running his hands along the inside of the capsule. "Think, Haze!! Where in the hell is the control panel switch?"

"Oxygen level is currently at point five. This is Erin Wise from your MIT experiment team. It's been a pleasure working with you on Project Gliese 581. Aloha, the top is about to open," Erin's voice cheerfully quipped.

"No! Cancel! Stop! Don't pop the top," Ash ordered, trying to think of a vocal command that would stop his impending death.

His hands shot up, abandoning his attempt to activate the control panel. His fingers splayed across the clear glass of the escape capsule as if attempting to hold it in place. All he could see beyond his hands was an inky blackness dotted with stars.

Ash drew in the last deep breath of air in the capsule. He desperately held onto the life-giving mixture inside his lungs. He wanted to prolong every nano-second of his life. The sound of the locks disengaging along the sides of the capsule echoed around him, sending an uncontrollable shudder through him as if the devil was running his bony fingers across a chalkboard. A second later, the top popped open and rose. Frigid air poured into the climate controlled capsule, wrapping its icy fingers around him. His eyes bulged as he fought the need to release the breath he was holding and draw in more.

Ash's hands reached up and released the straps holding him down. If he was going to die, he would damn well enjoy the feeling of floating weightless in outer space while he did so. In all honesty, he was surprised that his blood had not already frozen in his veins and that his lungs had not ruptured.

Pulling up into a sitting position, Ash released his death grip on the edges of the capsule… then frowned. He wasn't floating. It was freezing, but… he experienced worse while skiing in Colorado.

The overly loud sound of his breathing echoed around him. The stream of warm air he exhaled formed a long vapor trail in the cold air around him. Ash drew in a tentative breath, and was surprised at the clean, freshness of it. He shook his head in amazement.

"I'll be damned! Thank you, MIT and NASA! Erin, my beautiful college nerd, you were right! I swear if you were here now, I'd kiss you," Ash choked out on a laugh.

He blinked and took a long, assessing look around him. The capsule had landed in a desert about a mile or so from a mountain range. The landscape looked like part of Arizona or West Texas. A shiver ran through him when a stiff breeze swept across the capsule.

"How the hell did I get back to Earth? I didn't think these things could last that long," he muttered, twisting to gaze around the other side.

He raised a hand to touch the lump on his temple. It was still there and very tender. His fingers grazed the edge of a long, thin cut. There was no way he could have been unconscious for over a year. These things weren't designed to function more than a few weeks, if that long. He lifted his gaze to the sky again, and froze. As he drew in a deep, shuddering breath, his stomach clenched in dismay. There were two moons.

"Aw shit, so much for Texas," he muttered, running a trembling hand down his face.

* * *

An hour later, Ash folded the rest of the parachute into the capsule. It was too bulky and heavy for him to carry. He stripped everything else of use from the inside of the capsule.

"First aid kit, thermal blanket, extra coverall, emergency rations, water…," Ash murmured as he did an inventory.

He carefully packed each item into his lightweight backpack, then pulled a large knife from its nylon sheath, unfolded it, and cut off a two-by-two meter section of the parachute. After refolding the knife, he slid it back into the sheath at his waist and wrapped the section of material around his head, covering his mouth and nose so only his eyes were visible. Almost immediately, he felt some relief from the biting cold.

Ash then grabbed the top of the capsule and pulled it shut. For several long minutes, he stood looking out over the desert. He turned in a slow circle, trying to get a bearing on his location. He was still trying to wrap his head around the fact that he was on an alien planet.

"I feel like I need to be skipping along a yellow brick road singing 'I'm off to see the wizard'," he said with a grimace before he focused on the range of mountains in the distance. "I sure hope to hell the natives are friendly."

..*

Kella Ta'Qui slid her blade along the thick skin of the guard's neck. She released the limp body and stepped back into the shadows, scanning the area to make sure there were no more surprises. The guard must have been patrolling the outer perimeter. He had been further than she expected from the tower and hidden from view among the rocks.

They had startled each other when she stepped around the outcropping where he had taken refuge from the rain. She had recovered faster, kicking the laser rifle out of his hands, but he had countered with a stab to her side. The fight had been short, but vicious.

Blood dripped from the wound in her side. Kella slid her fingers into the small pouch on the belt around her waist and pulled out a medicated patch. She pressed the cloth to her side. Heat flared against her skin, drawing a soft hiss from her. Activated by her blood, the chemical in the cloth cauterized the torn flesh and temporarily stopped the bleeding. She would have to wait until she returned to her ship to do a more permanent treatment.

She bent and stripped the uniform off the guard's body. The uniform was too big, but by slipping it over her clothing it helped her look bulkier. She fastened her own belt under the one she had taken from the guard to keep the clothing in place. Next, she pulled the guard's helmet off, slid it over her head, and adjusted the view inside. After checking to make sure her black hair was hidden inside the helmet, she picked up the laser rifle lying at her feet and checked to make sure it was charged and working properly.

Once she was satisfied the uniform would adequately conceal her identity, Kella activated the computer inside the helmet. A quick scan gave her the information she desired. She turned her attention to her next target. The guard was standing on the bridge several meters above her current position.

She used the crevices and large boulders in the rocky incline to conceal her presence. She turned her head in slow, measured movements. The sensors in the helmet scanned the area. She paused when she saw a series of red security beams crisscross the front entrance of the tower above. She would deal with them once she cleared the two guards standing on either side of the beams.

Kella climbed up the last stretch of rocks, using the bad weather and darkness to help conceal her presence in the otherwise open area. Sprinting, she crossed the uneven ground and used the bridge to conceal her from the guards above. She knelt and prepared for the next part of her mission. Slipping on a pair of magnetic hand grips from her belt, she adjusted them before she activated the power. She stood up and lifted her arms over her head. The magnetic fields reacted to the electrical charge in the grips and her body rose off the ground as her hands were pulled to the underside of the bridge.

Swinging from one hand to the other, Kella moved under the line of soldiers patrolling the bridge. She would never have made it unnoticed through all of them without the magnetic grips. In the end, she would only need to make it through the security grid near the entrance. At least, that was what she thought until she saw the large conduit where the electrical and water lines entered the tower. It would be a tight fit, but it would get her inside.

Her arms felt like lead by the time she reached the end of the bridge. Kella paused, staring up through the metal slats as a dozen soldiers walked in formation out of the tower. Once they passed, she took advantage of the noise from their boots stomping on the metal slats and the closing of the doors to release the magnetic grips and drop down onto one of the large pipes. She bent forward, barely catching herself when she slid on the damp, curved surface. Her gaze flickered to the side. The tower complex was positioned hundreds of kilometers above the rocky surface of the planet. If she fell, there would be nothing to stop her descent.

Kella pushed up, ignoring everything around her, then crossed the short stretch of pipe to the opening. She climbed inside and began crawling. Her gaze flickered to the different command functions inside the helmet. She narrowed in on the night vision mode, activated it before she switched to the schematic of the tower downloaded into the helmet.

Reaching the end of the crawl space, she slid down behind a cluster of storage barrels. Her eyes narrowed when she saw someone move in the shadows on the other side of the open area beyond the barrels. Her lips tightened before she forced her body to relax. The sound of an alarm alerted her to the fact that security had been informed of a breach.

Kella waited until a large group of soldiers ran by before stepping out. She adjusted the uniform and walked at a brisk pace to the lifts. Stepping inside, she turned, holding her weapon in front of her. The other assassin started across the open area, heading in the direction she had just vacated. Kella raised the weapon she was holding and fired, striking the man in the side just as the doors to the lift closed.

"Bridge," she ordered.

The lift quickly ascended the long center support column. Kella checked the weapon before bracing it against her shoulder in preparation for the doors opening. She widened her stance when the lift slowed to a stop. The moment the doors opened, she began firing. Within seconds, the six people inside the bridge were no longer a threat.

She stepped out of the lift, turned her attention to the thick metal doors to her right, and pulled a small disk from her belt. She tossed it at the doors as she stepped to the side. The flashing light sped up before the small chemical pack exploded, coating the doors in a film that super-heated the metal. Kella stepped closer and fired once at the doors. That was all it took for them to explode inward.

Stepping through the smoke, she aimed her weapon at the two individuals inside. The caustic smoke had them coughing into their sleeves. Kella focused on the first male, her finger tightening on the trigger.

"Enough! Stand down, mission complete," a loud voice ordered.

"Now, assassin," the voice of her handler ordered.

Frustration and indecision poured through Kella. Her finger trembled on the trigger. With a curse, she lowered her weapon and stepped to the side.

"My mission was to eliminate them," Kella stated.

"You have achieved your mission," her handler stated.

Kella shook her head. "They are still alive," she retorted.

"Yes, Kella, and they will remain that way. Your mission is a success. You are ready."

Kella turned when she heard the voice of her mentor, Tallei. She reached up and removed her helmet. She knew her eyes were flashing with rage as she glared at the two men.

"They are still alive," Kella stated in a slow, even tone.

Tallei stared at her. The single black pupil that returned her gaze showed no emotion. Kella barely saw the hand that moved. The two men behind Kella collapsed to the floor, two dark scorch marks marring the center of each man's chest.

"Your mission is complete," Tallei stated before lowering her laser pistol. "You have a new assignment waiting for you."

"When do I leave?" Kella asked.

"Immediately," Tallei replied. "You will be briefed on the mission after you have departed."

Kella bowed her head. She started forward, pausing when her mentor didn't step aside so she could pass. The tall, thin Turbinta pushed back the hood of her charcoal gray cloak to reveal her face. A maze of scars crossed the older woman's pale green face. Tallei's left pupil was white, while the right was as dark as a black hole except for the slight dot of red reflected from the overhead lights.

Kella's smooth, forest green skin and clear, dark brown eyes were a sharp contrast. While she and her mentor were both Turbinta, the name did not refer to their species as much as it did to what they were – assassins. Kella did not know or care what species she was. She had long since accepted that it didn't matter. She was taken as a child by Tallei to be mentored in the ways of the Turbinta, and that was who she was now.

"Do not fail this mission, Kella," Tallei said.

Kella heard the warning. She knew that an assassin who could not complete a mission was of little use and a threat to the reputation of all Turbintas. If Kella failed, and survived, Tallei would come after her. Bowing her head in acknowledgement, Kella waited until Tallei stepped to the side.

She returned the way she came, ignoring the soldiers who had returned to their posts. This tower was used for the final training session of the assassins. The soldiers would be sent for reconditioning. Their failure to stop the assassination of the two members at the top of the tower was unacceptable. Each move Kella had made would be reviewed and analyzed. Then, additional measures would be taken to make it more difficult for future students in training.

It wouldn't matter to Kella. A satisfied smile curved her lips. She succeeded where the others had failed. She lived. Her gaze moved to the body of the man she shot. She didn't know him. He came from another tribe on Turbinta. If she had not killed him, he would have killed her. It was the way of their kind. They lived by the code of the mission: kill or be killed. There was only safety within your own tribe, and there was no guarantee even there that one might not be killed out of jealousy or fear.

She strode out of the tower, crossed the bridge, and began scaling the side of the cliff back to her ship. It took her almost two treacherous hours due to the pouring rain. The rocks were slippery and minor avalanches forced her to detour several times. After climbing down the last few meters, Kella staggered forward and activated the back platform of her ship. She stumbled up the platform into the cool, dry interior. Pressing her hand against the platform control button, she was thankful it closed all the way, especially since it had a history of sticking.

Only when she was safe did she lean against the door and release her tight hold on the pain piercing her body from the wound in her side. From the amount of blood dampening the outer uniform she not only ripped the wound open again, but it was deeper than she realized.

Pressing one hand against her side and the other against the cold metal of the door, she pushed off and stumbled across the cargo bay. Her spacecraft was a small, converted freight hauler. She purchased it with the credits she earned working at the local bar Tallei owned, serving those brave enough to venture into the Turbinta region.

"Ah, assassin's blood, how could I have been so stupid!" Kella hissed when she stumbled again.

She focused on her feet as they carried her down the short corridor to her bedroom. After stepping into her cabin, she unhooked both belts, peeled the guard's uniform off and kicked it aside. It was a little more challenging to pull off her black, form-fitting top. Spots danced in her vision and she gritted her teeth to keep from passing out. After tugging it over her head, she tossed the blood-soaked shirt to the side.

A violent shiver ran through her. Kella knew it was a combination of shock and the frigid air inside the freighter. Her fingers trembled as she pulled the small medical kit off the shelf. She pressed the release and the case opened. Inside was everything she would need to take care of any minor injuries. She hoped this was minor enough. Visions of the scars marring Tallei swept through her mind as she reached for the injector. She inserted a small vial into the end, pressed it against her stomach, and pulled the trigger.

A shudder of relief flooded her when the pain began to subside. Bowing her head, she drew in long, deep breaths and waited. A rueful smile curved her lips when she thought of her mentor. Kella had not learned how to find that place inside herself yet where she could cut off the pain. She remembered Tallei telling her about the many times she had to repair her body without the help of medication, including the time when her eye was pierced by another assassin's blade during a mission.

Kella discharged the vial, tossed the empty container onto the bed, then returned the injector to the kit. Next, she ripped off the patch she placed over the wound earlier. After tossing it aside as well, she picked up a small cauterizing wand from the medical kit, and held the ragged edges of skin together with one hand while she ran the wand over the wound with the other.

A small amount of smoke brought the smell of burning flesh to her nose. The combination of smoke and burnt skin made her gag. She would have looked away if she could, but she didn't have that luxury. Instead, she held her breath for as long as she could while she sealed the skin.

Fine beads of sweat glistened on her brow despite the coolness of the air around her. Her upper body was coated with fine bumps and she had to lock her knees to keep from collapsing. It took several minutes to ensure that the wound was sealed and no longer bleeding. She covered it with a clean medical patch that contained both a painkiller and medicine to help her heal faster.

She focused on cleaning up the area, replacing the wand in the medical kit, throwing away the empty vial and old medical patch, and carefully replaced the kit back on the shelf. Once the area was restored to its tidy condition, she pulled off her boots and removed her bloodstained pants. She quickly dressed, pulling on a long, thick black sweater over the thin top that restrained her breasts, another pair of black, leather pants, and slipped her boots back on. She would toss the clothing into the cleaner unit on her way to the bridge.

"*Tallei's tit,* she is going to be furious with me," Kella muttered when she realized that almost four hours had passed since she'd left the tower.

As if reading her mind, the communicator on the side table pinged. Kella grabbed the bloodstained clothes in one hand and reached for the communicator with the other. A glance told her that the instructions for her mission were still waiting to be received. A second communication showed that Tallei was not impressed with her tardiness in responding to either of them.

Kella strode down the corridor, pausing only to place her clothing in the cleaner, before hurrying to the bridge. After sliding into the pilot's chair, she began preparations for her departure. Within minutes, she had programmed her destination into the navigation system, strapped in, and was lifting off the large, flat surface near the bottom of the tower. Her hands tightened on the controls, steering the vessel through the narrow canyon before breaking free and increasing power to the main engines.

She breathed a sigh of relief when she broke through the storm and upper atmosphere. Once she was in orbit, she activated the message with her mission details. An image projected in front of her.

"Assassin, you have been assigned an urgent mission. A foreign capsule has landed on Tesla Terra. Your task is to locate the contents and deliver it directly to Lord Andronikos – preferably alive; but dead, if necessary."

Kella studied the map of the planet. Tesla Terra was in the northwest quadrant. It would take her at least three days to get there. She would locate the capsule and scan it for information, then search the Spaceport on the other side of the mountains. Someone was bound to have some information.

Chapter 2

Ash stretched and stifled a groan at the stiffness in his joints and muscles from sleeping on the hard ground. He walked to the opening between the boulders that formed the entrance of the cave and peered out into the fading sunlight. It would be almost an hour before he could leave his shelter.

He gazed out over the barren landscape, waiting for the sun to go down over the horizon. The narrow collection of boulders in the middle of nowhere became his temporary sanctuary. The journey he started on two nights ago quickly turned into a fight for survival. Everything had been fine until the sun came up the morning after he arrived, and he had started to fry – literally.

He had once been in south Texas along the Rio Grande during the height of summer, and decided anyone crazy enough to try to cross over had to either be insane or part lizard. But that was nothing compared to what it was like here. Before he found this small rock outcropping, he had pulled on the second set of coveralls and placed the backpack on top of his head to help give him added shade. It had not helped much – his skin still began to blister from the heat. By the time he had stumbled upon the cluster of boulders, he was in agony.

A small entrance where one boulder had fallen over onto the others revealed a tiny, hidden oasis. The dramatic temperature drop had been a blessing, but the discovery of a small pool of water bubbling up from the ground proved to be heaven. He had shed his clothes and bathed his scorched skin in the nearly icy water. He had been amazed when the blisters on the backs of his hands shrank the moment he plunged them into the shallow basin.

He spent the rest of the first day and all of the second day trying to plan a more efficient trek. He ventured out last night, but decided to stay put when he saw several faint lights heading in the direction he came the day before. Using the binoculars in the survival pack, he had switched on the night vision. Ash had counted at least five separate vehicles which looked like something out of a Sci-Fi movie heading in the direction of the emergency pod he abandoned. Several hours later, his fears were confirmed when he watched them load the capsule between the machines they were riding on.

It looked like nighttime travel was going to be his only option for more than one reason. Until he knew what in the hell he was dealing with and where he was, he would become a flea on a shaggy dog's butt. He just needed to find the shaggy dog first.

"Tonight," he murmured to himself.

Ash turned away from the entrance, and rechecked his inventory. He only had another two days' worth of rations. Thanks to the spring, he had plenty of water at the moment. He hoped there would be more water sources once he reached the mountains.

He lifted a hand to touch the wound near his left eye. The cut was sealed, but it would take at least a week or more to heal completely. He would probably be sporting a new scar. An assessment of the rest of his body turned up a few more abrasions and an assortment of bruises. Still, considering that he was alive, he would take the scrapes, bumps, and bruises any day. It would just be another fantastic tale of woe to impress the ladies with, he thought before he sobered again.

"Not that I'll ever see home again," he murmured under his breath with a sigh.

He grabbed his clothing and pulled his uniform on, then the extra coveralls. Already he could feel the temperature outside starting to drop. He shook out the scrap of cloth he had cut from the parachute and tied it around his head the same way it had protected him before. After shouldering the pack, he waited the last few minutes until it was safe to go outside.

"Time to ditch this joint," he muttered under his breath.

Ash focused on a bright star over the mountains. He would use it as a reference point. He pulled the straps on and fastened them across his broad chest, then took off at a steady jog. If there was one thing he could do, it was run – and run and run. He had always enjoyed it, appreciating the runner's high that came when he was in the zone. He would need that skill if he was going to make it to the safety of the mountains by first light. If he did not find a place out of the brutal sun, the only zone he was going to be in was the dead zone.

A light breeze flowed behind him, giving him a tail wind. He drew in deep breaths through his nose and released them through his mouth. The head cover would help conceal any vapor. By the third mile, he could feel his body getting back into the groove of running. His mind wandered, taking in the region even as he kept his guiding star in sight.

Almost two hours later, Ash slowed to a walk as he approached a winding dirt road that he could see eventually led to the mountains. He drew in deep breaths, placed his hands on his hips, and turned in slow, steady circles to glance in all directions. It was almost like coming to a fork in the road – which way should he go? One way led to the shelter of the mountains. The other way led away, presumably to a settlement. The question was: Which way *might* be a shorter and less arduous journey?

He needed to get to his intended destination – finding shelter before the sun rose. The problem was either direction could have inhabitants who may or may not welcome an alien visitor.

It was impossible to tell which way would be the better choice. Indecision tore at him before he realized that he did not have much of a choice. If he wanted protection from the sun, he would have to head in the direction of the mountains. More confident, he reverted to his original destination, this time following the road headed in that direction.

The night wore on and Ash continued alternating between jogging and walking at a fast pace. He took a ten minute break every hour and a half and drank just enough of his precious supply of water to keep the worst of his rapacious thirst at bay. The road curved around, running parallel to the mountains until it suddenly veered toward them.

Ash was shocked when he rounded a section of rock and discovered the entrance to a massive tunnel. The glimmer of lights at the far end held him paralyzed for a moment before his brain kicked in, and he realized he was about to have company.

His gaze swept over the area, searching for a place to hide. There was an overhang to the left of the entrance, and he sprinted toward it, climbing on the pile of debris left over from the construction of the tunnel. He pulled himself up and rolled to the side. His fingers groped for the clips holding the backpack on, and once he found and released them, he shrugged the pack off, pushing it to the side so he could lay flat. This would be his first chance to see what he was facing.

Sweat beaded on his brow as the seconds turned into minutes. The sounds grew louder before the first in what turned out to be a long caravan passed by him. Ash's eyes grew wide and his left hand moved to the knife in the sheath at his waist.

If the two moons and strange transports hadn't convinced him that he was nowhere near Earth, much less Texas, the large beasts carrying supplies were enough to make him realize he had traveled over the rainbow.

The animals moved in a long line. They were as tall as an elephant, but had the face of a Triceratops. Each of the horns, two horns above each eye and one centered just above its nose, had to be at least three meters long. The creatures were a dark red with a thick, leathery hide. They were each laden with heavy loads and moved along with slow, lumbering steps. Behind each beast was a sled that hovered above the surface of the ground with a native walking behind each sled.

There was also an alien positioned to the side and one in front of each animal. The aliens were humanoid, with two arms and two legs, and they walked upright. Their vehicles and sleds indicated that they were intelligent and had an advanced culture. They were covered from the top of their heads to their booted feet with loose clothing; their goggles shielded their eyes and helped to keep the cloth covering their faces and hair in place. Their bodies were tall and slender. Ash pulled his binoculars out of the case attached to his waist and focused the lenses on the aliens. Up close, he could see dark red skin peeking out from under their long sleeves as they moved.

He shifted his focus to their faces. He couldn't see any details of their features other than some kind of nose under their coverings, a humanoid jaw and cheekbones, and two eyes. He zoomed in to peer at their goggles, but even with the light of two moons, he couldn't glean much information about their eyes.

He'd need to find clothing that was similar to theirs and mimic the way they moved. The color of his skin would be a problem, but if he didn't let anyone get too good a look at him, the clothing would conceal who he was. He could do Halloween dress up as well as the next person.

He continued to watch the line, mentally taking notes as each person passed by him. The line seemed to go on forever before it finally ended. It reminded him of some of the super long trains back home that used to go by his house when he was a kid. After the caravan moved off along the road, Ash hesitated for another few minutes, his gaze scanning the area for stragglers, and then he reached for his pack, secured it onto his back, and climbed down from the ledge.

From the side of the entrance, he peered into the darkness and listened for anyone else. Once he was confident he was alone, he stepped into the cave. Picking up his pace until he was jogging again, he headed to the exit, nearly two kilometers from the entrance. The last thing he wanted was to get trapped in the tunnel when another group came through. From the intense heat of the day, he imagined that the vast majority of travel was conducted at night. He would have to be twice as careful. If they were accustomed to traveling at night, they would be more adapted to seeing in the dark as well. Life just became a little more exciting.

He slowed when he reached the other end of the tunnel. Bright moonlight flooded the entrance. He pressed against the wall, blending into the shadows when he reached the opening. The road wound down, sloping into a desert valley on the other side. Lights glittered like stars along the valley floor.

Ash gazed in awe at the city below him. He blinked, fascinated by the maze of buildings rising from the sands. Lights glittered like fireflies across the valley floor. His eyes widened when he saw spaceships of all different sizes lifting off and landing. He followed one with his eyes, his mouth gaping open in astonishment when it suddenly flashed upward through the atmosphere. Without thinking, he raised his right hand to pinch his left arm.

"I've fucking died and gone to utopia," he murmured under his breath.

For the first time it really hit him that he was alive, on an alien world, and all alone. A wave of grief struck him at the thought of how much Josh, Sergi, Mei, and Julia would have loved to see this. This is what they had lived and breathed to discover. Another world – with intelligent life – to experience first-hand. The geeks back at NASA would be drooling all over their consoles if they could see what he was seeing.

"Shit, Josh, you don't know what you are missing, man. I wish you were here to share it with me," Ash whispered, returning his gaze to the city.

He shook his head in regret before he began making his way down the side of the mountain. In his mind, he ran through the things he would need to do first. He needed to find clothing, a weapon, and a place to hide before sunrise. If he was going to survive, he needed to learn a lot about this world and the people in it, and he would need to blend in – not an easy thing to do when you were a black man from another planet.

"They sure as hell didn't have a simulator for this back on base. It's a good thing I like playing video games. Those nerds never knew what they were creating, but they sure the hell weren't too far off in their imaginations!" Ash muttered under his breath, jogging up to the edge of a farm of some type. He didn't see anyone in the field.

He knelt behind a small boulder and assessed the buildings. There was a light tan structure that appeared to be a house. It reminded him of some of the adobes in Arizona and New Mexico. If people stayed inside during the day and went out at night, there was a chance it would be empty. Ash didn't see any lights on inside. Maybe some aliens didn't need light. Except if that were true, the city would have looked dark from the mountain, wouldn't it? So they were either not here, or they were sleeping. The row of outbuildings might have something of use inside as well. His eyes caught sight of some clothing hanging from a rope tied to a suspended line.

Item one: check, he thought with satisfaction.

Rising up, he strolled over to the line as if minding his own business. The first rays of light were beginning to brighten the sky. If the alien farmers were like the ones back home, they would be early risers – or would that be opposite here? Rising with the sunset? As if on cue, a light shone through a window of the house. They weren't night owls then.

Ash quickly gathered several articles of clothing from the line and kept walking toward one of the outbuildings. He tested the door of the first building before he noticed a control panel next to it. Disappointment filled him when it refused to open. This wasn't a simple lock that he could pick, and a sliding door was impossible to kick in.

He moved to each one, discovering the same thing. Slipping behind the last building, he shrugged off the backpack and started to take off the emergency coveralls he wore over his uniform. He grimaced when the sleeve caught on a piece of sharp metal. Jerking it free, he ignored the soft sound of the material. Kicking the coveralls aside, he slipped the long robe over his uniform. Next, he replaced the scrap of parachute he had used as a head scarf with the long piece he had taken from the line. He wrapped it around his head and over his face like he had seen the men in the caravan wearing it, then he bent and stuffed the coveralls and parachute material into his backpack.

Now he needed to find a weapon. He had his knife, but he would like something a little more alien – or less alien, depending on one's perspective. Something that wouldn't stand out here, in any case. He rose to his feet, and pressed against the side of the building when he heard voices talking in a language he couldn't understand. Glancing around the corner, he saw a woman walk out to gather the clothes off the line.

He was about to make a run for the house when the door next to him beeped. He jerked back, and waited. It took several seconds for him to realize that the doors must be on some type of timer and were set to unlock at a specific time.

"Sweet!" Ash muttered, grinning under his face-covering.

He swept his hand over the panel and the door slid open. This shed was the furthest from the house and the door was angled toward the open fields of dry rocks. He would have to work quickly if he wanted to escape unseen.

He stepped into the dim interior, and started when the ceiling lit up. The interior walls and ceiling were curved, giving the space a wide, roomy feel. He glanced around the inside. There were several different pieces of large equipment, which looked like they were used for plowing, and various other farming implements. What they grew in the sand and rocks, Ash had no idea, but they must be able to grow something.

Cabinets and shelving lined the interior. He walked around the farm equipment and began pulling cabinets open, careful not to disturb anything if he could help it.

In the third cabinet, he discovered a pair of goggles similar to those the aliens were wearing last night. He pocketed the goggles before moving on to the next cabinet. Inside there was an assortment of large farming blades and smaller knives. He took a small one and left the others. Frustrated, he was about to give up when he glanced at the farm equipment again.

"Why is it when you are looking for something it is always either the last place you look or right in front of you?" he mumbled in exasperation.

There were two weapons on the large machine he was circling. A small pistol type weapon was on the dash and there was a long rifle in a holster behind the seat. A sense of regret pulled at him as he took both weapons. He hated taking something for nothing.

A grin curved his lips. Shrugging off the pack on his shoulder, he reached in and pulled the coveralls out. He ripped off the Project Gliese 581g patch showing the countries represented and left it on the seat. It wasn't much, but he bet no one else on this planet would have a patch like that.

"You can bill the Project Manager," Ash chuckled as he stuffed the coveralls back into his bag and zipped it up.

After picking up his pack again and shouldering the weapons, he strode back to the door. He paused, glancing out of it. The woman was yelling at a young boy who was staring back at her with a puzzled expression. Ash waited until the woman's back was turned and he couldn't see the boy before stepping out and quickly closing the door behind him. He slipped around the side of the building and took off

Chapter 3

Kella walked farther away from the burned out vineyard, her boots leaving prints in Tesla Terra's soft soil without making a sound. She scanned the wooded area, making sure she was alone before she stopped at the edge of a large depression in the bed of leaves and debris. It was obvious that something had landed here. The deep, rectangular impression in the muck was still evident, as well as the tracks of the Legion soldiers, half covered by a new layer of leaves.

"What did they find? What could have been so dangerous that the Legion Director would hire the Turbinta to retrieve the contents when he has an entire army at his fingertips?" Kella murmured with a frown.

She reached out and ran her gloved fingers along the edge of the impression. Her head tilted to the side when a shimmer of silver caught her attention. She stood and walked over to the bush that held the foreign object. She bent and carefully pulled the branches aside. A section of reflective cloth had tangled on the thorny twigs. It took her several minutes to release the material from the bush's avaricious grasp, but her persistence paid off when the material came free

She assessed what she knew so far. The burned out vineyard she had visited first belonged to the de Rola family; owned by none other than Jemar de Rola, a former Knight of the Gallant. His name and one other, Jesup, were on the grave markers. There were still two more members of the family missing, though: Cassa and Packu de Rola. Kella had heard tales of the Knights of the Gallant, but that was all they were as far as she was concerned – tales. It was hard to believe these 'Knights' had ever been capable of protecting the galaxy.

Kella discovered very little about the other two de Rola family members except that they were well respected by the merchants they traded with at the Spaceport. There was another lead that she needed to investigate – Hutu Gomerant. It was only natural to conclude that the remaining de Rola family members would seek help from the only other Knight of the Gallant still alive, even if the man did sell junk for a living now. The few inquiries she made before coming to the vineyard and forest were met with silence and suspicion. She would have to gain her information in a different way.

Several hours later, Kella had secured the land transport in her freighter docked at the spaceport. She changed into the feminine clothing of a Tesla Terra merchant. Staring at her reflection, she focused on her skin. It changed from the forest green to a sand color. She left dark spots along her forehead and down her neck. Her ability to change her appearance was one of the reasons Tallei had chosen her as a student. Satisfied that she would appear, at least at first glance, as a native of the planet, she carefully hid her laser gun and blades within easy reach.

Kella exited the freighter and activated the security system. As an added precaution, she murmured to one of the street urchins who frequented the area hoping for a handout. She showed the boy two credits.

"Guard my freighter well and inform me if anyone goes near it. I will give you one credit now and one when I return. Lie to me, boy, and I will slit your throat," she instructed, holding the coin just out of his reach.

"I don't lie," the boy informed her with a stubborn glare.

"Make sure you don't and you might live longer. I will return in a few hours," Kella replied with a curt nod before dropping the coin in his outstretched hand.

She turned and strode away from the landing ports back toward the city. Her dark brown eyes missed nothing as she made her way through the thick crowd of traders. She slowed when she neared the residence of Hutu Gomerant. Slipping into the shadows, she watched from across the street.

There were at least six guards present, unusual for a junk trader. Kella's eyes narrowed when she saw two figures step out from behind the house. Her eyes widened in surprise when she saw the face of one of the men. He was different from any she had seen before. Unusual enough to be the owner of the capsule who was of such interest to Lord Andronikos? She did not believe in coincidences. The

Knight of the Gallant had led her to her quarry, just as she had suspected he would.

Hutu said something to the male and he nodded before pulling the hood over his head. She waited several precious seconds before she stepped out of the shadows and began to follow them. A short time later, the two men disappeared into a local bar. Kella wanted to follow them, but knew that in her current garb she would stand out. Instead, she was forced to find a spot where she could observe the entrance without drawing attention to herself.

Time passed slowly before the two men reappeared. Kella straightened from where she was leaning against the building and began following them. Her fingers closed around one of her knives. She would need to get closer to make sure that she had a clear area to strike at the old man. He was of no further use to her. She would need to kill him and wound the other. Picking up her pace, she veered to the left when several men fell into step behind her target, cutting off her chance to make a clean kill.

"I have a ship…."

"Legion forces…."

"Must leave soon…."

Kella stopped where she was and watched Hutu and the strange man walk back to Hutu's residence. If they planned to leave, she needed to stop them, or at least know where they were going next.

Those who lived around the landing ports were not as closed-mouthed as those in the marketplace. For a few credits, she should be able to discover where Hutu's ship was docked. There would be more opportunities now that she had found her target.

..*

Close to an hour later, Kella tossed aside the metal bar she had used as a hammer. The small piece of metal she found was now wedged firmly in the locking gear securing Hutu's spaceship. It would take time to loosen it. While they were working on it, she would strike.

She looked up quickly and glanced at the door. The sound of the lock disengaging echoed through the repair bay. Kella hurried to hide behind one of the curved stone pillars and drew her laser pistol. Switching it to stun, she leaned her head back against the pillar and listened.

Kella cursed when she heard multiple footsteps. There were more than just the two men. Peering around the stone pillar, she saw Hutu. Frustration bit at her when he hurried to the opposite side of the ship.

The strange man she was to capture and take in was behind a woman. Kella suspected she had found the two missing members of the de Rola family. She lifted her pistol and aimed. Her finger hesitated on the trigger. A silent curse escaped her.

Something didn't feel right. She didn't know what it was, but her gut told her now was not the time to strike. She had learned to trust those instincts. Tallei had told her that was what made her such a good assassin. All Kella knew was that those feelings had saved her life more than once during her years of training.

"You two get the supplies on board," Hutu instructed from the shadows of the platform. "Pack, you get the locks on that side."

Kella watched from behind the pillar. Tonight, she would observe her target and those with him. She had placed a tracker on their ship, just in case this encounter did not go according to plan, so she would have no trouble following them.

There would be a better opportunity at another time. She watched as the young man worked to free the lock she had jammed while the other two carried supplies onto the spacecraft. Her attention snapped to the main doors when she heard shouting. On the other side of the doors, loud yells to 'open up' and thumping alerted Kella to the presence of the Legion forces.

"Pack, I need you to help me get the engines going. It is time to go," Hutu ordered above the sounds of the Legion troopers.

"This lock is stuck," Pack yelled back as he worked to free the gears of the lock.

"Go help Hutu. I've got this," the strange man said with a jerk of his head.

Kella watched the man look around. He spied the same metal pipe she had used as a hammer a short while ago. Her gaze narrowed on him when he stood up and hurried closer to her. Now was her chance. Her finger hovered on the trigger of her laser pistol, but once again, something stopped her. Perhaps it was the expression on the woman's face, or the look in the man's eyes when he turned to Cassa de Rola. She watched him return to the locking device.

"Let me help," Cassa de Rola said, hurrying to help him.

Kella watched the two working together. For a moment, she saw a different man staring at a woman with a dark green face – a face that she could barely remember. The man was smiling at the woman who bent to pick up a basket filled with food. The images were so clear, she felt as if she could reach out and touch them.

She flinched, coming back to the present when a loud boom echoed through the repair bay. The door exploded inward. Kella didn't stop to think. When the man and the woman began firing at the Legion troopers, she did as well, cutting the soldiers down as fast as they entered. She barely had time to escape before Hutu's spacecraft lifted off.

Exiting through the hole she had created on the back side of the building, she turned and watched the spaceship disappear. A moment of confusion swept through her before she pushed it aside. She had hesitated – unfamiliar feelings and memories were interfering with her mission. It was imperative that she resist such weakness. Tallei would beat her within a breath of her life if she knew about Kella's failure – if she was feeling lenient. Failure in the field was supposed to result in death.

Shaking her head in self-disgust, Kella pursed her lips and turned to head back to her freighter. The Legion would lock down the Spaceport and Kella needed to be long gone before that happened. She was not worried about finding out where Hutu and his passengers were headed. The tracking device she planted on the spacecraft would guide her right to them.

Tossing a credit to the young boy watching the freighter, Kella boarded and prepared for departure. From the communications filtering through, she had been right. The new Legion commander was issuing an order to lock down the Spaceport. Like Kella, dozens of ships were doing a mass evacuation.

Once she was far enough from Tesla Terra that she did not have to worry about a Legion boarding party, she activated the tracking device. It took several minutes to register, the delay confirming the other ship had gone to light speed. The moment their trajectory came through, Kella input the likely destinations. A smile curved her lips when she saw the edge of the Torrian home world as a possible location.

"Where do you go when you are running and looking for a place to hide? Home…," Kella murmured, quickly programming the same position into her computer.

"I will not fail this time, Tallei," Kella whispered, taking the freighter into light speed.

Chapter 4

Ash sank back into the shadows of the alley and stretched his legs out. Today had been a good day overall, he thought. He had collected enough food to last him and his new friend Kubo a couple of days if they were careful. It also gave him a chance to scope out more of the area.

"The Legion looks for someone," the old man sitting next to him muttered.

Ash glanced at the clouded eyes of the man in surprise before he shook his head. He didn't know why Kubo could still shock him. He had become acquainted with Kubo almost two weeks ago. He knew from the cloudiness in his eyes the man was blind, but Kubo didn't miss anything – including the fact that Ash had pilfered a few pieces of fruit from a stand near where Kubo had been standing. The next thing he knew, Kubo had followed him back to the alley where he proceeded to knock Ash on his ass – both figuratively and literally. Ash absently glanced toward the end of the alley.

"Who is the Legion?" Ash asked, watching two soldiers walk by.

"They follow the orders of a crazy man," Kubo stated, holding out a withered red hand and wiggling his fingers in the direction of Ash's brow.

Ash grunted and handed Kubo a piece of fruit he had taken from a stand several streets over.

"I hope you paid the merchant for this," Kubo muttered, accepting the treat.

Ash grinned. "Of course," he lied.

The late afternoon snack had become a routine for them. He was still amazed that the two of them could understand each other. He had heard Kubo talk to others, but he spoke a different language when he did that. Kubo was teaching him the Torrian language, but it was slow going because Ash had a hard time wrapping his tongue around some of the sounds.

Ash remembered the muttered curses that had escaped him when he hit the ground during their first meeting and his shock when Kubo answered him. One of the first questions Ash had for Kubo was how the hell was Kubo able to understand him. It seemed incredible that they spoke the same language.

..*

Kubo had touched his ear. "I listened to you talk under your breath. You talk a lot. Every species are taught the universal language spoken by the ancients. Some are more adept at using it than others. You speak it differently from any I have heard before. I am Kubo. What are you called?" Kubo had asked with a humorous chuckle.

"Universal... Ancients... I... Whatever you say, old man. I'm Ashton Haze, but everyone calls me Ash. Can you tell me where in the hell I am?" Ash had finally responded, rising to his feet when Kubo had removed the long, twisted stick from his chest and motioned for him to stand.

Kubo had leaned against the long stick and tilted his head in curiosity. "You are on Torrian," he had replied.

That encounter had begun a beneficial partnership between the two men. Kubo guided Ash around the city and shared his meager dwellings while Ash supplied them with food. Kubo had explained the strange disappearance of the majority of the residents during the day. They moved underground, which is where Kubo lived, and left the crowded marketplace to the alien visitors of their world during the hottest part of the day.

..*

Ash watched several more soldiers march by the entrance to the alley. Over the last few days there had been an increase in what appeared to be the local military. He assumed they were military from the way they were dressed and the way they moved, but one thing was very clear – no one liked them.

Ash narrowed his gaze when two of the soldiers stopped one of the merchants. They were questioning the man, but they were too far away for Ash to make out what they were saying. All he knew was he had to make several detours when he discovered checkpoints where they were searching people.

He discovered that acting like a crazy homeless person worked just as well here as it did back home.

Whatever worked, he would take it, because some of the shit he had seen almost scared the piss out of him. There were creatures, both big and small, here that were straight out of Fright Night at one of the theme parks.

"They search for a long box that fell from the sky," Kubo murmured, tilting his head to the side with a frown. "They are offering a large number of credits for it…. and for the contents inside."

"Yeah, well good luck with that," Ash retorted, reaching up and adjusting the goggles covering his eyes to a more comfortable position.

"They will not find it. If they do, they will be dead. Come, it is best to retreat underground where they will not come," Kubo chuckled, rising.

"What makes you think they won't come underground?" Ash asked, standing and following Kubo.

Kubo walked slowly down the alley in the opposite direction of the soldiers. As usual, Kubo took his time answering Ash's question. It wasn't like it was a particularly difficult one. Ash decided Kubo just liked to jerk his chain. He started to open his mouth when Kubo hit him in the shin with enough force that it knocked him sideways.

"Clumsy, boy. His feet are as deformed as his brain," Kubo stated loudly. "He is only good for carrying my purchases."

"Identify yourself," a soldier ordered.

Ash had lowered his head to rub his shin when he saw the tops of the soldiers' boots. The curse he was about to utter turned into a guttural snort. He followed it with an exaggerated Frankenstein's Igor shift.

"They are just Torrian beggars. This one is blind and the other one doesn't function correctly. Let them pass. They can give us no information," a soldier stated.

"Yes, sir," said the soldier who had stopped them.

"Move along," the other soldier ordered.

Kubo nodded and turned. Ash's lips twitched when the two soldiers jumped back to avoid getting hit by the long staff Kubo was holding. The smile turned to a grimace when he felt his shin protest the abuse. He was going to have a talk with Kubo about better ways to alert him. Crippling him wouldn't help if he needed to fight or run.

They were silent until they stepped behind one of the vendor's carts. The cart shielded the alley behind it. To most, it would look like a dead end. It wasn't until they reached the end that Kubo held up a crystal tied around his neck and flashed it. Ash resisted the urge to jump when the ground opened up in front of the wall and a staircase appeared.

He followed Kubo down the staircase, glancing over his shoulder when it sealed again. Four Torrians stood on either side with weapons while another operated a video surveillance system. Ash quickly looked away when one of the men glanced in his direction. Kubo had barked out a sharp word to the men the first day he brought Ash down here. Ever since then, it appeared every resident in the city had kept their distance, even as their eyes followed his movements.

"It is time, Ashton Haze, that you told me about your journey to my world," Kubo stated several minutes later as they walked beside an underground river.

"Now?" Ash asked in surprise. "I thought you told me to keep my origins to myself."

Kubo glanced in his direction with an amused expression. "I did, but now I think it is time you told me," he replied.

Ash followed Kubo across the short but wide bridge, glancing at the other aliens passing by. Ash noticed there were more guards and armed citizens than before. There was also a tension in the air that was missing this morning.

He noticed that the residents were bowing their heads when Kubo passed. He turned in a circle, trying to decipher the subtle changes from this morning. Something was off.

"What's going on?" Ash asked with a suspicious voice.

Kubo chuckled again. "Follow me," he ordered.

Ash noted they were heading in a different direction from the humble hole in the wall that Kubo took him to the first night they met. Each time they entered the underground city, it was through a different entrance. Even the vendors up top moved around to the point that he seriously doubted he would be able to recognize a way in.

Primitive, yet complex dwellings, much like the homes of the Ancient Pueblo Indians, were built into the walls of the cavern. Ash followed Kubo when he crossed the large, sparsely populated cavern to the far side. There was nothing there but the uneven red and tan rocks that made up most of this planet from what he could tell. Ash started in surprise when the wall of rock suddenly moved. The opening revealed a set of stairs carved deeper into the ground. Reaching out, Ash trailed his fingers along the uneven surface as they slowly descended. Thick grains of quartz glowed in wide veins, sparkling and lighting the staircase from some hidden source contained within the rock.

"Seriously, Kubo, what the hell is going on?" Ash asked, trying to decide if he should find a way out of the underground maze or trust his gut to stay and find out what the hell was happening. His gut was generally pretty accurate – generally, but he never had to test it on an alien world before. "I don't like going into a situation without knowing what the hel…."

Ash's lips parted in surprise when they stepped into a large cavern filled with activity. This was a lot different from the dwellings above. Shops and homes surrounding a park in the center took his breath away. Large trees rose almost fifteen meters above to the top of the cavern, and thick, bluish-green grass grew on each side of the river that cut a path through the center of the city. The staircase exited near the waterfall that probably originated from the river in the upper cavern.

"Welcome to the ancient city of Torrian," Kubo murmured with a wave of his hand.

"Wow! What the hell were we doing upstairs when you have this down here?" Ash asked in awe.

Kubo chuckled. "We guard our cities well. Only a few outsiders have ever seen the true cities beneath our sands. It keeps us safe. We built above for the visitors who come and to shield us from those who would try to attack. Torrians are not as stupid as the Legion would like to believe we are."

"I'd say not," Ash agreed, stunned at the sophistication of the city he was staring at.

A young Torrian hurried forward and bowed his head in greeting. "General Gomerant, Commander Dungway has sent a message," the man said, glancing curiously at Ash.

Ash frowned. 'General Gomerant'! What the hell did the young man mean by General – as in *military* General? Ash turned to stare at the old man who he thought was practically homeless. That cunning son-of-a-bitch had conned him.

"General?" Ash asked with a raised eyebrow.

Kubo grinned again. "This way, Ashton Haze," he chuckled.

Ash shook his head and pointed a finger at the old man walking away from him. "You, old man, are the one who has a lot of explaining to do," he called out behind Kubo.

Kubo's laughter rang out around the cavern, drawing the attention of those close enough to hear him. Many of the residents gazed at Ash with curiosity, while others held a measure of suspicion. Ash lifted a hand up and pulled the goggles up to rest on his head scarf before he yanked the bottom cover down. Several people stopped to stare at him. He flashed them an easy grin, knowing it didn't quite reach his eyes. His right hand fingered the long rifle hanging from his side. He sure as hell hoped he would not have to shoot his way out of here.

Chapter 5

Alarmed communications between freighter captains near the planet described unexpected boardings and arrests. Kella listened to the chatter and learned that General Landais' Battle Cruiser had taken up a position near the third moon of Torrian. He was one of the Legion Director's most feared generals. Those wary of being boarded were either avoiding the area or coming in from the far side of the planet. They stayed low along the mountains and desert regions, using known smuggling routes that were dangerous to traverse.

Kella took their advice, and was lucky enough to find a berth at a landing region just outside the city. It was outside the regularly checked area, so she was less likely to receive an inspection.

The tracking device she mounted on Hutu's ship had either malfunctioned or disintegrated upon entry and she was left with no idea where Gomerant's spaceship landed. Kella glanced over her shoulder, taking note of the landmarks to memorize the location of the landing port. She had to leave her freighter here, but unease ate at her. Legion forces were massing around this area. Yet, it would have been more dangerous to have landed farther outside the city. Kella had no doubt that the desert raiders would have her ship dismantled before the end of the first night.

* * *

Kella moved smoothly through the crowded Torrian marketplace, covered from head to toe as one of the freighter pilots who frequented the city. She was ignored by those busy with their daily activities.

She had traveled to three cities in almost as many days, but this was the right one. The former Knight of the Gallant had been seen in this city. She had investigated everywhere within the city's boundaries for nearly five solar days now, but she knew she was close. She had the description and location of the merchant willing to sell directions to 'Sandsabar', Hutu's mysterious hideout. She spotted the merchant's cart first, then among the crowd, she saw her informant. Kella sidled up close to him and placed the credits in his hand.

"Sandsabar," Kella murmured in his ear.

The man looked her up and down before jerking his head to a building farther down the street. "Down there," he replied, his voice deep and rough.

"*Ta tie,*" Kella replied, giving the standard Torrian thanks.

The man grunted at her and turned to a customer. Kella strode forward, scanning the area. The Sandsabar appeared to be a busy drinking establishment. Her gaze paused on two men standing near one of the huge desert beasts. One of them was stroking the long tusks of the creature. He looked innocent enough, but his gaze scanned the crowd.

Kella turned her back to him, but not before she saw the second man caressing the blaster by his side.

She continued her surveillance of the area. Three of the merchants in front of the establishment were more interested in observing the people walking by them than selling anything. Another woman near a fountain had already filled the same container four times. Kella turned and continued past the building. The roof of the Sandsabar was dome shaped, which meant she couldn't use it. A quick scan told her that wouldn't be a good option anyway. Guards patrolled the rooftops of the two buildings on either side.

Kella walked past several buildings before she turned and retraced her steps. Taking the front steps into the Sandsabar, she paused to allow her vision to adjust to the dim interior. Crowds of traders, pilots, and laborers mingled in small clusters. She spied two men leaving one of the small booths in the corner and strode over to it.

She had no sooner slid into the seat than one of the waitresses came over. Kella ordered a Torrian liquor and sat back in the corner. Her hand automatically moved to the laser pistol strapped to the inside of her arm. She adjusted it so that she had a firm grip on it.

A wry smile curved her lips. This was tame compared to the bar Tallei owned. Kella had lost count of the bodies and body parts she'd been forced to clean up over the years. She nodded to the waitress and tossed a credit onto the tray when the woman placed her drink on the table.

"You want anything else?" the waitress asked in a barely audible voice.

Kella glanced up at her. "How is the food here?" she asked.

The waitress smiled, showing off a line of crooked teeth. "Good, and safe. Devona is picky about what is served," she replied.

Kella nodded. "Bring me the house special, I am hungry," she ordered, tossing two more credits on the tray.

The waitress's eyes widened and she eagerly nodded before turning away. Kella knew she would get excellent service. She had overpaid for her drink and her meal. Tallei would have lashed out at her for doing that. It was not the way of the Turbinta. It would cause her to be more memorable than if her behavior had been unremarkable, but Kella knew how hard the work was and hadn't missed the fact the waitress was with child. She justified her actions as a fair trade for receiving fresh food that wouldn't leave her sick, or in the extreme case, dead.

Nearly two hours later, Kella was rewarded for her patience when Hutu Gomerant stepped into the bar. Kella nursed the drink in her hand, watching as the owner of the bar eagerly hurried toward Hutu. Her gaze followed them to a booth near the back. Devona nodded to the men sitting in the booth next to the one she and Hutu slid into, then sent a meaningful look to the bartenders behind the bar. Tallei had given Kella that same look many times before. They were bracing for hostile company.

* * *

"You think I'm *what*?!" Ash exclaimed.

He lifted his hand to push against his chin. He knew his mouth was hanging open. It tended to do that when he was shocked speechless.

"You are an Ancient," Kubo repeated.

"I'm thirty-two," Ash automatically responded, running a hand down his face.

Kubo shook his head and sat forward in his chair. "You know the number of planetary cycles since your birth is not what I am talking about," he chided.

Ash's hand dropped to his side. "Come on, Kubo. You expect me to believe I'm some Knight of the Gallant Order, magically returned to help defeat the Legion and restore order to the galaxy? If you do, I have a bridge in Brooklyn I'd love to sell you," he retorted.

Kubo sat back in his seat. "I do not need a bridge from Brooklyn. The galaxy needs the Knights of the Gallant," he stated, folding his hands around the handle of his cane.

Ash looked suspiciously at Kubo. "How in the hell did you come to the conclusion that I'm this… this… Gallant Ancient?" he demanded, throwing his hands up in aggravation.

"You came through the gateway built by the Ancients, fell from the sky, speak the old language, and the Legion is searching for you and the others. It matters not what the rest of us believe, though it will help our cause. What matters is that Director Andronikos believes it," Kubo replied with a wry grin.

"This sounds like something out of a comic book," Ash groaned, slumping in his seat before he sat up when Kubo's words sank in. "Wait a minute! Did you say others? What others?"

Kubo raised an eyebrow at him. "Did you come alone through this gateway you told me about?" he asked.

Ash clenched his fist to keep from shaking his finger at the old man. He'd discovered the guards standing off to the side didn't take kindly to him doing that. Instead, he glared at the blind man in aggravation.

"No, I told you there were five of us. Has anyone else been found?" Ash demanded.

"Perhaps," Kubo responded with a shrug. "The Legion searches for the others. General Landais wants you found. His men search the desert near Commander Jubotu Dungway's base."

"Well, good luck finding anything. I saw five guys hauling my escape pod away, and what do you mean 'perhaps'?" Ash asked, folding his arms across his chest.

"There may be another," Kubo stated. "Hutu is here. There were three others with Hutu; Cassa and Packu de Rola and a stranger from another world."

"Where?" Ash asked, his eyes narrowing on the serene face in front of him.

Kubo raised a hand. One of the guards near him stepped forward and murmured in his ear. Kubo nodded and the man stepped back.

"My son, Hutu, meets with others in the resistance. He meets with Devona at the Sandsabar," Kubo finally stated.

"Your son!" Ash exclaimed, dropping his arms to his lap.

"Yes, my youngest," Kubo replied.

Ash stood up. If there was a possibility of finding more survivors from the Gliese, he wasn't going to sit by and wait. Josh, Mei, Sergi, and Julia, they might not all be dead. One of them was with Hutu at the Sandsabar.

"I want to go to the Sandsabar," Ash stated.

Kubo nodded. "I suspected you would. It would not be wise for me to be seen there. I will send someone to guide you," he paused, then continued in a suddenly old and tired voice. "You must not draw attention to yourself, Ashton Haze. The rebellion needs you and the others alive."

Ash was about to argue again about who they thought he was, but instead he just sighed. The only thing that was truly important right now was finding the others. Kubo murmured to his guard, and Ash wandered off, trying to curb his impatience while he waited for the guide.

It didn't really matter what these people called him and his crew. The rebellion needed them alive, and this 'Lord Andronikos' and his Legion wanted them dead. It was a helluva spot to be in.

Hard to believe that an Air Force brat from New Jersey was someone's idea of a legend. *The Ancients, the Knights of the Gallant Order, protectors of the galaxy, come on!* He had grown up running the streets and getting into more trouble than he could clearly remember. It all pretty much blurred into the same shit. *Hell, if it wasn't for Josh and my grandmother, I would probably be in jail instead of flying planes.* He was no knight in shining armor, that was for sure.

Ash meandered toward the stairs and slowly walked down the narrow steps, lost in thought. It did sound like fiction, just how *much* his life had changed. How did a human wind up in another galaxy, who knew where in the universe, only to be mistaken as some prophesied knight? He would have had a better chance of being sucked up in a tornado and deposited in Oz.

Stepping out onto the lower section, he looked down over the large open area. Unconsciously, he lifted his right hand and pinched his left arm. He winced from the pain and shook his head. So much for hoping he had just been dreaming the last few weeks. "Erin, where in the hell did you and the rest of the nuts from the MIT department send me?"

"Who is MIT?" a feminine voice asked.

Ash started in surprise before he turned. A young Torrian woman stared back at him with a curious expression. A slow smile curved Ash's lips. Who knew that red might be the new sexy? Turning to face the woman, Ash's gaze moved over her face. She had large, dark brown eyes he was sure he could drown in. Her face was a long oval shape with a small nose and mouth. Dark swirls, like tattoos, curved across her forehead and down along her cheeks and throat before disappearing under her tunic. His gaze moved back to her eyes. Long, dark lashes made them really stand out.

"Just the geeks who programmed my escape pod, darling. My name's Ashton Haze, but everyone calls me Ash. Who might you be?" Ash asked, stepping closer and raising her hand to his lips.

The woman looked back at him with a slightly amused expression. Ash gave her one of his sexiest smiles, reluctantly releasing her hand when she tugged on it. She shifted the long staff to the hand he just kissed.

"I am called Natta, not darling. Father has asked me to guide you to the Sandsabar," she said.

"Father…," Ash started to say, glancing back with a frown at the stairs he just descended before he looked back at Natta. "How many kids does Kubo have?"

"Forty," Natta replied. "Come."

"Forty! Are you shitting me?" Ash exclaimed in shock, turning to stare up at the open balcony where Kubo stood. "Geez, no wonder the old man is blind!"

Natta's laughter told him that she had not only heard what he said, but that she understood his meaning. Ash might have actually blushed in embarrassment if he hadn't been so shocked. Well, not really, but forty…! Shaking his head, he turned and followed his new guide.

"Were you serious?" Ash asked when he caught up with Natta.

Natta glanced out of the corner of her eye and laughed again. "No, but it was worth it to see your face, Ashton Haze who likes to be called Ash," she replied with a mischievous grin.

"Well, I'll be damned. Aliens with a sense of humor. What next? Chewy and the Munchkins doing a sing-along?" Ash muttered.

Chapter 6

Ash followed Natta through the crowded streets. The nights were always busier than the days. Kubo had explained that many of the desert dwellers came to the city to do their trading after the sun went down. They completed their business at night in order to avoid the hottest part of the day on their return trip home.

After his first horrendous experience with the blistering heat, Ash could appreciate the need for that precaution. He would have practically killed to have had a set of these clothes that first day. It was nothing short of amazing the difference the clothing made in protecting his skin from the damaging rays.

Between the clothing and the goggles, he didn't have any trouble during daylight hours now. Kubo had explained that the clothing was made from plant fibers that had a natural sunscreen. The texture of the fabric also allowed it to breathe, cooling the body. In a unique process, the Torrian fabric makers also added additional protection made from the flowers of the same plants.

"Our red skin is also conditioned to the intense heat. Your skin, even dark as it is, will blister," Kubo had observed.

A shudder ran through Ash as he remembered the torture of the blisters. If he hadn't found that group of rocks and the shallow spring nestled among them, he had no doubt he would have been a burnt corpse. At the moment, he was enjoying the cool, almost chilly breeze flowing through the tunnels that were cut deep into the mountains.

"The tunnels help cool the valley," Natta explained when she saw him shiver, thinking that he was cold. "During the day, the heat rises. The tunnels are very long and are cooled by the water that seeps from them. When the dry air blows in from the desert, it is channeled through the tunnels, cooled, and flows down along the valley floor, pushing the heat up. It becomes trapped and helps to keep the city at a temperature where even in the height of the day, many visitors can venture out of the buildings."

"I noticed that. It's a lot like nature's own air conditioning system," Ash joked.

"I do not know this air conditioning system," Natta replied, stopping to stare at Ash with a critical look. "You must cover your face better. There is a gap between the goggles and your head scarf. We do not normally wear either at night in the city. Hopefully, you will be mistaken for a sand dweller."

Ash adjusted the head scarf. He waited until Natta was satisfied before he dropped his hands back to his side. His hand wrapped once again around the grip of the laser rifle he had taken.

Natta's eyes widened, and she reached out to grip his arm. Ash started to glance over his shoulder to see what startled her, but she hissed and gripped his arm tighter to keep him from looking back. She wrapped her arm around his and pulled him back the way they had come. When they passed a section of merchant carts, she pushed him behind one. Raising a slender finger to her lips, she nodded to a large group of Legion soldiers that were stopping people.

"Something is going on. Stay here while I find out," she ordered in a barely audible voice.

"Natta," Ash protested, his fingers curling around her arm to stop her.

Natta shook her head. "I will be fine, Ashton Haze. If we get separated, the Sandsabar is at the end of the street and on the left. It is the only building with a domed roof. Do not enter through the front. Instead, take the alley in the back, but use caution if you do. Legion forces will be out front," she instructed.

"Won't the soldiers search the back alleys?" Ash asked with a frown.

Natta shrugged. "Perhaps, but very few merchants would travel the darker, more isolated alleys. It is not safe. At night, raiders and cutthroats from other worlds search for the unsuspecting to rob or kidnap. It is too easy for someone to attack you at night. There is safety in numbers, so those who are smart stay to the main streets. If you need to travel that way, be prepared and check carefully before you move. Perhaps, it would be better to return to the underground city."

"No, I need to know if any of my friends survived. I can handle a dark alley, Natta. I've been down a lot of dangerous ones in the past," Ash assured her.

Natta hesitated for a moment, searching his face before she reluctantly nodded. "I will go see if I can discover what has happened."

Ash dropped his hand when she stepped back around the thick curtain of cloth hanging on display. He moved a couple of steps to the left so he could peer through a gap in the fabric. Natta was pretending to look at some merchandise while moving closer to the soldiers.

She was almost to a small group of them when they suddenly turned and began pushing through the crowd. They were heading in the direction of the Sandsabar. Natta fell back against the table across from him when another group of soldiers ran by in formation.

"Shit!" Ash muttered.

Turning on his heel, he cut through the back of the shop. Pausing, he carefully opened the back door. Several buildings down, he counted two… four… five movements. The sounds of yelling out front told him that whatever was happening was heating up.

"Ash!" Natta hissed, coming up behind him.

Ash turned with a muted curse, his hand freezing just shy of Natta's neck. He clenched his fingers and let his hand drop to his side. She stared at him with wide, startled eyes.

"Don't… It's not a good idea to startle me, Natta," Ash warned. "What's going on?"

"General Landais is here!" she replied.

"That's the Director's guy, right?" Ash asked in exasperation.

"Yes. He is very, very dangerous, Ash. You must not let him see you. I must get you to safety. We should return to my father," Natta whispered in an urgent tone.

Ash reached up and touched Natta's cheek. "No, sweetheart. If this guy is after your brother – and possibly one of my friends – I need to go. I'm a soldier too, Natta, and a damn good one. Go warn your father that General Landais is here. I hope your brother can handle himself," Ash said, turning away.

"The guards will have already warned Devona. She will send Hutu and any others through the factory behind the Sandsabar. There are many ways to exit the building that will lead them away from the Legion forces. Here, take this. It will get you in through the doors," Natta instructed, reaching up and removing the crystal from around her neck. "Be safe, Ashton Haze."

"No worries, darling. I was born for trouble," Ash retorted with a wink.

"My name is not…," Natta started to say before she shook her head and watched Ash step out of the building. "I hope Father is right, Ashton Haze. Our world and many others need to know there is hope against Andronikos and his forces."

..*

Ash moved cautiously along the wall, pausing in the shadows and listening for any sound of movement or voices. Shooting the rifle would not do him much good in a close fight, but he could still use it as a weapon. Thanks to Josh's dad and his grandmother, he and Josh had taken martial arts classes after they were caught spray painting railroad cars. Ash didn't know which parental figure he had been more afraid of, Josh's dad or his own grandmother, when they came to the police station to pick them up. Being handcuffed at the age of eight had convinced Ash that it was not the way he wanted to spend his life. His grandmother's silence and the disappointment in her eyes was his undoing. When Josh's dad appeared three days later with a brochure on Judo and Taekwondo classes available on the base, his grandmother had taken one look at him and signed the permission form.

For the next nine years, he and Josh attended classes seven days a week, practically through every rain, shine, and sick day. It helped that the two of them did it together. After getting their asses handed to them on a platter during their first competition, they had made a deal to keep training until they were the best.

Those extra years honed their senses and toned their bodies. Ash quickly learned the ladies liked seeing 'his moves' both in and out of the bedroom. He wasn't opposed to flexing a little muscle if it meant a nice night of mad, passionate, no-holds-barred sex. Of course, it helped that he wasn't as picky as Josh was either.

Ash sent a small thanks to both Josh's dad and his grandmother for not giving up on him and pushing him to be the best at whatever he did – well, the sex wasn't part of it, but they didn't have to know that. He was ready for whatever came his way. Ash felt his muscles tense before he forced them to relax. There were two men on either side of the alley. The only way past them was going through the middle.

Drawing in a deep breath, he forced everything from his mind, searching for his center of balance. Once he found it, he stepped forward and waited. He didn't have long to wait.

Just as Natta warned him, the two men moved in on each side of him. Ash didn't wait to ask what they wanted. Swirling the rifle in his hands, he slammed the end of it into the throat of the man to his right. He didn't pull his punch. The blow knocked his attacker back into the shadows of the building, leaving the man choking and gasping for air.

Twisting around in a graceful arc, Ash knocked the legs out from under the assailant coming at him from the left. This one was more nimble than the other attacker. He hit the ground and rolled back to his feet, a long blade in his right hand.

"You'll be a good one for the fight rings," the man snarled.

Ash shook his head, understanding about half the Torrian words the man spoke. "I'm a lover, dude, not a fighter. Just ask the ladies," he replied in English deciding it was too complicated to speak it in Torrian.

"You can be sold for that, too," the man retorted, charging him.

Ash blocked the jab and struck the man's chest with lightning fast moves before bringing the butt of the rifle up under the man's chin in a tooth-shattering blow. He finished his offense with a crushing strike to the attacker's right cheekbone. Ash grimaced when he heard the bones snap. That was going to hurt like a son-of-a-bitch in the morning.

The second attacker crumpled at his feet, knocked out from the blow. Ash turned back to the other man who he had throat punched. He was still lying on the ground holding his throat. Soft, muted sobs escaped him. Ash muttered a curse. He hoped the blow wouldn't kill the guy. He didn't relish dealing with the alien version of a court of law.

"Aw shit, I don't need this," Ash groaned, walking over to the guy and pressing the rifle against his chest. "If you are fucking pretending, I'll blow a hole through your chest, do you understand me?"

The man nodded. Ash knelt down next to the attacker. It wasn't until he looked more closely that he realized the 'man' was really just a boy. The boy's face was long and thin, as if he hadn't had much to eat. His face was a powder white with dark orange and black stripes on it. His white hair was short and spiky. Yellow, cat-shaped eyes stared up at him fearfully. Shaking his head, Ash touched the boy's throat with gentle fingers. The boy winced, but remained perfectly still.

"You'll be alright, son. You may be drinking liquids for a few days, but you'll live. You need to find better company to hang out with than that jackass over there," Ash told him with a reassuring pat on the boy's chest.

The boy's eyes widened and he nodded. Ash stood up and glanced over at the other attacker. There was no doubt that the man was an adult and not a greenhorn like the kid. With a shake of his head, he glanced down the alley. The other three he saw had disappeared. He didn't know if the fight scared them away or if they decided to take their nefarious activities someplace else.

Ash gripped the rifle close to his side and took off at a sprint down the alley. He was still several blocks from the Sandsabar if he had to guess. Three buildings down, he veered to the side and into the shadows. Dozens of Legion troopers were beginning to swarm the buildings and alleys.

"Shit," Ash whispered, backing up into the doorway and watching.

His stomach clenched when he saw the first body they carried out. It was only when they passed through a shaft of moonlight that he saw the Legion uniform on the man. His gaze moved to the top of the building when he saw lights flash from above. It would appear whoever they were looking for had escaped.

Ash fumbled for the door behind him when he noticed a group of soldiers glance in his direction. They wouldn't be able to see him in the shadows from their location, but at the rate they were moving, it was only a matter of time before they would be able to. He mouthed a silent curse when he realized it was locked.

The sudden memory of the crystal Natta had given him flashed through his mind. Reaching into his pocket, he pulled it out and waved it in front of the control panel. Almost immediately he heard the click of the lock disengaging, and the door slid open. He stepped backwards and watched the door close.

He decided it was time to blend in with the crowds again out front. He might be able to get close enough to the Sandsabar to discover what was going on. Ash pocketed the crystal and adjusted his head scarf and goggles again. Clutching the rifle against his side, he strode toward the front of the building. The merchant looked at him, held up a hand, then waved for him to move out into the crowds once several Legion soldiers walked by.

Ash didn't know how the Torrians' network was so good, maybe they had some kind of communication system set up, but he could feel the gazes of the other merchants following him as he walked past them. He paused across the street from the Sandsabar. A Torrian woman was standing in stiff defiance, glaring at the soldier in front of her.

Ash turned when the crowd suddenly became quiet and parted, as if by some invisible force. He couldn't help but think it looked like waves parting in a biblical sense when the line of soldiers stood at attention in two perfect rows, and the crowd around them came to a standstill. A tall, dark-haired man in a black uniform strode forward. Ash saw enough generals and admirals during his military career to know this was someone of high rank and importance.

This must be none other than the dreaded Count Landais, Ash thought.

Okay, maybe classifying the guy with the same lines as Count Dracula might not be the best way to think of him. After all, Ash was on an alien planet so anything could technically be possible. It also didn't help that while Hollywood tried to glamorize the guy, all the history books pretty much stated the same thing – you didn't want to piss off Dracula if you wanted to live.

General Landais must have felt Ash's intense gaze on him because he slowed to a stop and carefully scanned the crowd. Ash stepped behind a slab of hanging meat. He hoped the guy didn't have x-ray vision. Several tense seconds passed before Landais turned and continued walking by the woman and the group of soldiers and entered the Sandsabar. Only when Landais was gone did a collected sigh of relief echo through the crowd.

"Wow! And I thought Admiral Greenburg was a hardass," Ash muttered under his breath.

Ash stepped out from behind the cart. Several merchants were excitedly talking and waving their hands in the direction of the bar, but looking out toward the edge of the city. He frowned, trying to follow what they were saying.

From the little he'd learned over the last couple of weeks, it was difficult, but not impossible. Only about a dozen words filtered through to his limited vocabulary – stranger, ancient, spaceship, escape, and port or landing or something. Ash debated if he should say anything, then decided it was probably best not to with the large cluster of Legion forces. They were still trying to round up everyone who had been inside the bar. If they pulled his face cover and goggles off, it would be a no-brainer that he wasn't from around these parts.

Instead, he stayed in the shadows and began working his way through the thick crowd of people. He had been by the landing ports with Kubo one day during their excursions around the city. It was one of the few times when Ash had almost given himself away in his excitement to see the spacecrafts that were taking off and landing.

Ash would have given anything to take a tour of one of the ships. Kubo had promised that would be for another day. There were too many Legion forces around to attempt sneaking aboard one at the moment. Now, he was in a race to see if he could catch up with Hutu Gomerant and the mysterious stranger the men were talking about.

Chapter 7

Kella stumbled forward behind the building two streets over from the warehouse. She bit back the groan of pain that ran through her head and chest. She found her target, but he turned out to be more resourceful than she anticipated.

They fought. Normally that would not have been much of an issue, but he used moves that she had never encountered before. She also did not see who struck her from behind. If Tallei had witnessed the fight, she would have told Kella she deserved to die for not being better prepared.

All Kella knew was that she should have killed the strange man instead of trying to capture him. The next time she found him, she would. Tallei said 'dead or alive'. The Legion Director might prefer the male alive, but now that Kella knew there was more than one of them, she could always deliver one dead and one alive.

"If I survive," she muttered under her breath, falling back against the wall.

She barely made it out of the building before the Legion forces swarmed the factory. It would not take them long to discover that she had killed one of the soldiers. She had no choice. The soldier surprised her. He mistook her for one of the workers in the factory who had stayed late – until he saw her up close and realized that she was not a Torrian, but a Turbinta. He had attacked her, leaving her no choice but to defend herself.

Kella braced an arm against the rough stone of the building to keep herself from falling. The strange alien carried the Staff of a Knight of the Gallant. She read about them in one of the information disks left behind at Tallei's bar. She thought the stories in the book were just tales to amuse people.

Even Tallei had been silent when Kella asked about them. When she persisted, Tallei had taken the disk from her and thrown it away, telling Kella not to believe in mystical tales.

Kella had retrieved the disk from the trash and hidden it away in her small box of treasures, knowing that her secret collection was a betrayal of the Turbinta way, but unable to help herself, even as Tallei's lesson from long ago had surged to mind.

"A Turbinta must value nothing, Kella; to care leaves you weak and vulnerable. Your enemies will use it against you," Tallei's unemotional voice had filled her mind.

"But… what about you? I care about you, Tallei," Kella had whispered.

Tallei had responded by taking her outside and beating her until Kella felt sure she would die. When she could no longer move, Tallei had stood over her in the pouring rain. Kella had been barely conscious, but she would always remember the cold expression in Tallei's eyes as the rain fell around them.

"You are nothing to me if you are weak, Kella. Pick yourself up and get to work. If you can't work, you won't eat," Tallei had said in a voice as cool and calm as the rain.

Kella opened her eyes and winced as she pushed away from the wall behind her. She hadn't given up then, and she wouldn't give up now. A shiver of warning ran through her body, and she lifted her head. Three dark shadows were emerging from the alley across from her.

"It looks like we have a new fighter for the rings," one of the men chuckled.

Another one shook his head and spit on the ground. "It looks like this one just got out of one," he retorted.

It was the third one that chilled Kella to her bones. His dark eyes stared at her with a coldness that would rival Tallei's the day she had beaten her. Kella struggled to stand up straight. She slowly drew the blade at her waist.

"Look at her marking. She's a Turbinta. Just net her ass and lock her up before she recovers, otherwise we'll all be dead," the man with the cold eyes stated.

"A Turbinta! That's big credits!" the second man laughed.

Kella snarled and released the blade in her hand. The man jerked back several steps in surprise before he released a howl of pain and collapsed to the ground – the blade buried in his right shoulder. She cursed. She had been aiming for the center of the man's chest.

A snarl escaped the large man at her attack. Kella had already palmed another blade when a webbing of strong threads struck her. The force of it lifted her up off her feet and slammed her back against the wall behind her, knocking the wind out of her.

She fought to break free of the net holding her captive. The man with the cold eyes stepped forward and backhanded her across the face before he ripped the knife out of her hand and touched the tip to her chin. Kella could feel blood seep from her bottom lip and the sting of the knife piercing her chin.

"If you weren't so valuable, I'd slit your throat and leave you here to rot," he murmured.

Kella spit in the man's face. A soft grunt escaped her when he struck her in the stomach. The force was enough to push the air from her lungs. She reached inside, focusing on the techniques Tallei had taught her to push the pain from her mind. It was hard to do when he hit her bruised ribs right where the male from the factory struck her.

"I want to hit her, Con," the first man complained.

Con turned and waved the knife at the man. "Leave her face to me, Grange," Con ordered, walking over to the second man writhing on the ground. "Hold still, Tuprat."

"Don't…!" Tuprat screamed when Con reached down and jerked the knife out of his shoulder.

The man's scream barely registered in Kella's brain. The sound was muffled by her own mind exploding with pain when Grange's fist connected with her bruised ribs. It wouldn't take much for her ribs to break at this rate. She braced for the next blow when the second attacker suddenly spun away from her and flew into the other two men.

"You know, this is wrong on so many levels I can't even begin to list them," a deep voice stated.

Kella didn't know who the man was, but the relief from the beating was instant. If she could cry, she would have. At the moment, the only thing keeping her upright was the netting. Pain radiated through her body from her head down to her toes. Trapped against the wall, there was little she could do but hope whoever stopped the men wouldn't leave her here – or finish what they started.

He was dressed like a Torrian. Her foggy mind tried to pinpoint what was different about him, because despite his clothes, she knew he *wasn't* a native here. He was shorter and broader than most Torrians, at least the ones she had seen, but that wasn't what confused her. It took a moment for it to dawn on her. He spoke in the old language like the other man from the factory.

"Move aside Torrian, this Turbinta is ours," Con stated.

The stranger shook his head. "Well, you see, there's this little problem. A few, actually. First, I'm not a Torrian, second, I don't care what the hell you call her, she's a woman, and third, I've got someplace to be and you're keeping me from it," the deep voice responded.

Con frowned and widened his stance. "Who are you?" he demanded.

Kella forced her head up. She wanted to know the answer to that question as well. Her lips parted in warning when Grange suddenly came out of the dark.

The protest on her lips died when the man standing in front of her gripped Grange's outstretched arm. She watched the man twist Grange's hand and arm at an odd angle, deftly taking the knife from him. He didn't release Grange when Con attacked. Instead, he turned so that Grange took the blow Con threw.

The stranger released Grange when he crumpled, shoving the unconscious man toward the last attacker. Con tossed his partner's body aside, uncaring when Grange's head hit the stone flooring of the alley. Grange's body landed next to Tuprat who was still lying on the ground holding his shoulder. A loud hissing sound filled the quiet alley as Con drew in a deep, angry breath. The man in front of her appeared unconcerned, not flinching when Con started his attack.

Kella watched the stranger deflect blow after blow. The laser pistol Con tried to pull went flying before he even had a chance to raise it. The stranger moved so fast, she wondered if her foggy mind was to blame for not seeing it.

The moves were eerily familiar. Intense satisfaction flooded her when Con's head struck the stone wall next to her. She watched his eyes roll back in his head before he slid down to the ground. He didn't move again.

"Kill them," Kella ordered when the man turned toward her.

He paused before shaking his head and pulling a knife from his waist. "Uh… no," he said, sawing on the netting holding her to the wall.

Kella leaned her head back, trying to see behind the goggles and material covering his face. She frowned when he moved in and out of focus. Blinking, she tried to clear her vision.

"You must kill them," she stated, her voice slightly slurring.

The man chuckled and shook his head again. "You're a bloodthirsty little thing. I guess I would be too if those asswipes had used me as a punching bag," he muttered.

Kella leaned her head back, trying to will the world to stay in focus and her legs to support her. She still did not know who this man was or why he had saved her. Con had told him what she was. Every species in the known galaxies knew what a Turbinta was capable of and would sooner slit their own throats than chance having them alive.

"Hang in there, darling. I've almost got you free," he said.

"I… Watch out," she warned.

The unusual man didn't even bother to turn around. She watched him kick Tuprat, who was already off-balanced by the wound she had inflicted earlier. Tuprat stumbled backwards and fell over the inert body of Grange. The sound of his head hitting the hard surface of the alley echoed loudly.

"That… is going to hurt," the man said with a shake of his head.

"Who are you?" Kella asked in a barely audible voice.

The man wrapped an arm around her waist and held her steady when she started to collapse. He returned his knife to the black pouch at his side and slid his other arm around her knees, lifting her up against his chest. Kella groaned when the pain in her ribs protested the movement.

"The name's Ashton Haze, but my friends call me Ash. Knight in shining armor, romantic at heart, and royal pain in the ass, sweetheart. What's your name?" he asked in a distracted voice, first turning one way then the other.

"I am Kella. Where are you taking me?" Kella mumbled, laying her head against his shoulder and closing her eyes.

Ash released a deep sigh. "I'm damned if I know. I've got to find a way around the Legion forces, and I'd prefer not to have to kick any more ass tonight to achieve that goal," he admitted.

"There is a place not far from the city," another voice said from the darkness. "I can show you. You will be safe there."

Kella winced when she lifted her head. She started to protest, but was suddenly too drained. Tallei really would kill her. No assassin would ever be caught alive and held in a pair of strong arms, defenseless and weak. She felt the arms around her tighten before they relaxed when she groaned in pain.

"Hey, aren't you the kid...?" Ash started to say before his voice faded to a muted mumble in her head.

Chapter 8

Honestly, Ash didn't know what to think. He'd barely had time to hide again when another group of soldiers began stopping people and scanning them. He had threaded his way through back alleys along with dozens of others trying to escape the security net the Legion was closing over the city. His trek toward the spaceport turned into a game of cat and mouse.

Just when he thought he would be safe, he had come across the four in the alley in time to see Brutus the Butthead striking a trapped woman. There were a lot of things Ash was willing to look the other way for – but watching men beat up a woman was not one of them.

Ash warily followed the boy he struck earlier. They paused outside of the dark building on the outskirts of town. A loud sound distracted him for a moment. He turned his gaze to a freighter lifting off a short distance away before refocusing on the boy standing in the doorway.

Ash was torn. A part of him wanted to hand the unconscious woman in his arms over to the boy and take off in the hopes of finding Hutu. That hope was quickly fading with the passage of time and the increasing buildup of Legion soldiers.

Hindsight being 20/20, he realized he should have been better prepared for this mission. He would be the first to admit that attention to detail was never his strong suit. He was more of a fly by the seat of your pants type of guy which is why he and Josh made such a great team. Josh analyzed while Ash improvised. They always kicked ass up in the air because they were unpredictable.

"Abeni, that's your name, right? You'd better not be shitting me. I won't be forgiving a second time," Ash warned, staring hard at the boy.

"I…," Abeni started to say when an elderly voice behind him spoke.

"Je mi la tia pei, Abeni?" a woman called.

"Nia mi laya, Noma," Abeni replied, turning to face the woman when she peered out of the door.

"Comli, comli," Noma gestured.

"Noma says to come in," Abeni translated.

Ash nodded. "I figured that much out," he said, carefully shifting the woman in his arms.

Abeni stepped back and glanced around when Ash stepped past him. A moment later, the boy followed him inside. Ash glanced around the small room. It was sparsely furnished. Separating part of the room was a bright, multi-colored, striped curtain hung from a rope stretched across from one wall to another and tied to two thick hooks. Noma stood with it pulled back and motioned for him to place the woman in his arms down on the bed.

"Thank you," Ash murmured, stepping past her and gently lowering Kella to the bed.

"I will care for her. Abeni, bring food and drink for our guest," Noma ordered before she closed the curtain.

Ash shook his head. "I need to find someone. He might have gone to the spaceport. I need to see if I can find him," he said.

"I could take you, but it would not be safe at the moment. The Legion forces are everywhere. You saw how difficult it was to get here," Abeni cautioned in a quiet, hesitant voice.

"This is important. I have to find Hutu Gomerant," Ash groaned and yanked off his goggles.

Frustration burned in him at the delays. He didn't realize that he had also pulled the bottom of his head scarf off to reveal his entire face until he heard Abeni's indrawn breath.

"Are you the one the Legion is looking for?" Abeni asked.

Ash started to shake his head and stopped. Instead, he shrugged in reply. He honestly didn't know if he was the one the Legion forces were looking for or not. He doubted it, but that could be because they didn't know about him – yet.

"No, but I can't be certain of that. Why did you help me, kid? I almost killed you back there in the alley," Ash asked.

Abeni glanced toward the curtain. Ash didn't miss the boy's concerned look or the fact that he touched his throat. He could tell it must have hurt when the boy spoke. For a brief second regret washed through Ash before he pushed it away. If it taught the boy a lesson about who to hang out with, then a sore throat and an upset grandmother were a small price to pay. He knew that from personal experience.

"Because you did not kill me," Abeni finally admitted.

"Lesson learned," Ash replied with a nod. "Listen, do you know who Hutu Gomerant is?"

Abeni eagerly nodded. "Everyone knows of the legends of the great Knight of the Gallant. He was chosen by the Order of the Gallant to protect the people. It is a great honor," he said in a soft, scratchy voice.

"Well, I need to find him. He was supposed to be at the Sandsabar. There may be others with him. One of them looks like me, only with lighter skin," Ash said.

Ash watched Abeni press his lips together. Once again he glanced at the closed curtain. Ash could see the indecision in the boy's eyes. They both turned when the curtain pulled back far enough for Noma to step out from behind it. She had the same pale face with orange and black markings and yellow, cat-shaped eyes. Her faded eyes were clouded with worry.

"Abeni will go find the Knight. You must stay here," Noma instructed, turning and speaking in the language that Ash didn't understand.

Abeni bowed his head. "I will return," he promised, hurrying for the door while Ash looked on in confusion.

Ash started to follow Abeni, but Noma reached out a hand and touched his arm. He turned to look at her. Her eyes glistened with worry, but he didn't see any deception in them.

Noma dropped her hand back to her side and gazed up at him. "Neither Abeni or I will betray you, Ancient Knight. You must remain here," she said, waving to a small table. "Sit, I will prepare some food for you."

Ash gripped his goggles in his hand. He glanced at the door, then at the closed curtain before turning his attention back to the old woman. Noma reminded him a lot of his grandmother. She had that same quiet authority when she spoke that he couldn't quite disobey.

Releasing an exasperated sigh, Ash shrugged the rifle off his shoulder and walked over to the table. He propped the rifle up against the wall, dropped his goggles on top of the table, and pulled his head scarf off before sitting down. Absently shaking out the fabric, he folded it before setting it top of the goggles.

"Do you happen to know what the hell is going on and how everyone seems to know except for me?" Ash asked when Noma placed a cup of water in front of him. "Thank you."

Noma smiled and turned to pick up a small plate filled with fresh fruit, blue and orange cheeses, and the coarse bread that he discovered was surprisingly tasty. She walked over and set it down in front of him before stiffly lowering herself into the chair across from him. He glanced around the small room. Guilt tugged at him. It was obvious from Abeni and the home he was in that Noma and Abeni had very little for themselves, much less anyone else.

"Thank you," Ash said, picking up the smallest piece of fruit he could find and pushing the plate across to her.

Noma smiled back at him. "It does not take long for news to spread here. The walls have ears," she replied with a wave of her hand.

Ash popped the fruit into his mouth and scowled. "What did the walls hear?" he asked.

Noma glanced toward the curtain for a moment before she shook her head and turned back to face him with conflicted eyes. He reached over and picked up a piece of the cheese, hoping she would answer him with something he could understand.

"There is talk that the Ancient Knights of the Gallant have returned," Noma murmured. "They appeared and were scattered through the star systems."

Ash gazed back at Noma. "Did they say how many Knights?" he asked.

Noma shook her head. "I heard of one from Tesla Terra and that the Legion looks for one here. The word is there may be more, and the Director has offered a reward for the capture of them – dead or alive," she said, glancing at the curtain again with a worried frown.

"Nice," Ash muttered dryly before he followed her gaze. "What's wrong? Does she need a doctor?" he asked.

Noma looked at him again. "Where did you find her?" she asked curiously.

Ash shrugged. "Three guys jumped her in an alley several blocks from here and were using her as a punching bag. I saw what was happening and rescued her," he said.

"She is a Turbinta," Noma stated.

Ash shrugged again. "I know. It doesn't matter to me who or what she is. That doesn't change the fact that no man, much less men, have the right to beat a woman," he replied.

A small smile curved Noma's lips. "What is your name, Knight?" she asked in a soft, awed tone.

Chapter 9

Kella laid on the bed listening to the quiet conversation on the other side of the curtain. Her fingers absently played with the knife she had drawn from its sheath. She was shocked when she regained consciousness and found herself not only safe, but still armed with all of her weapons except for the two knives she lost earlier during her fights.

She turned her head to look at the curtain. It was closed, so they could not see that she was awake. Something warned her that the old woman who cared for her knew she was conscious when the man who saved her laid her on the bed. The woman's cold hands had trembled when she ran them over the tattoo on Kella's neck that marked her as a Turbinta. She would earn another one when she completed her first mission.

Her lips parted at his calmly spoken words. He didn't care – she was a woman. He did not see her as a Turbinta, an assassin, as – the lowest form of living creature. He saw her as… a woman.

Kella returned the blade to the sheath attached to her arm. Pushing against the bed, she winced, drawing in a deep breath against the pain and dizziness as she sat up. She silently slid her feet off the bed and braced them on the floor. Her right hand moved to her left ribs. She gently probed the area, assessing if any of her ribs were cracked.

After a minute of pressing and prodding, she decided they were just badly bruised. She had suffered much worse and lived. Her tongue flicked over her busted, lower lip. She traced the swelling, but again dismissed it as only a minor wound. Tilting her head to the side, she continued to listen to the quiet conversation.

The old woman called the man who saved her one of the Ancient Knights. A frown creased her brow. How was that possible? Tallei called them a myth – yet, this male spoke oddly, in the old language spoken on the disk and that was taught to each species.

She had once asked Tallei about the strange language and why it was necessary to learn it. Tallei had explained it was the universal language. The language was one that all understood, even if they did not use it on Turbinta except to communicate with the traders and pirates who came to do business.

This man spoke the language with a strange dialect, using some words which she did not understand, like darling and sweetheart. He also fought unlike anyone she knew, except for the man in the factory. If this stranger was like the other one, she could complete her mission by delivering him to the Director. She needed to find out if he came from a capsule that had fallen from the sky.

After rising silently to her feet, Kella adjusted her balance carefully as she waited for the vertigo to pass, then stepped closer to the curtain. She peered through a small gap in the opening, studying the face of the man who had saved her. Without the headscarf and the goggles, she could see his face clearly now. He was different from any man she had ever seen before, even Hutu's stranger.

Her gaze ran over his features. His hair was cut close to his head. It was black with tight curls. His skin was a smooth, creamy medium brown. His nose was broad and flat, and his lips... Kella's eyes widened when she felt an uncharacteristic response from her body. Her lips actually tingled. She raised her right hand and touched her fingers to them before dropping her hand with a scowl.

The only reason they were tingling was because of the blow she'd received, not because of the strange man. She fiercely glared as she continued to run her eyes over him. He had dark brown eyes and a crooked smile that made a curiously small indent appear in his cheek.

She grudgingly admitted she thought his jaw, covered with a slight stubble, made him look... attractive. The scowl on her face darkened, and she shook her head in disgust. What kind of assassin thought her target was attractive? The blow she received to her head must have been worse than she realized for her to forget all of Tallei's lessons.

A soft snort escaped her. Reaching out before she changed her mind, she yanked the curtain aside and stepped out. Both the man and the old woman rose from their chairs. Kella tossed her head – and promptly felt the world tilt.

"Whoa, darling, you shouldn't be up," the man said, wrapping a strong arm around her waist to steady her.

Kella tried to straighten, but the spinning in her head refused to cooperate. She stumbled a little when the man – Ash, his name flashed through the fog in her brain – led her to the chair he had been sitting in. Her left hand groped for the table and she used it to help keep her balance as she sank down into the chair.

"My name is Kella," she said, unable to think of what else to say.

The man's quiet chuckle washed through her. "Yeah, I remember that, and the fact that you can be a little bloodthirsty," he teased.

Kella blinked at him in confusion. "That is what I'm supposed to be," she said.

"I know, I know, you're a Turbinta," he replied, again playful instead of fearful or repulsed.

Kella started to nod her head, but decided it would not be a good idea. Instead, she turned to look at the old woman who stood to the side and behind Ash. The fear in the woman's eyes was what she expected. She blinked again, before turning her gaze to the food on the table. Her stomach growled.

"What species are you? You are different," Kella remarked.

She reached for the plate and pulled it toward her with a quick glance at the woman. Kella hoped some of the dizziness was due to her hunger. Stuffing several pieces of fruit into her mouth, she chewed them quickly before picking up the cup on the table, sniffing it, and draining it in one gulp. Almost immediately, she began to feel better. Satisfied that it was food she needed, she picked up a piece of the bread, laid a slice of the cheese on it, and bit into that.

"I think we might need some more food," Ash replied dryly.

Noma nodded, looking over at the bare cupboard. Kella caught the tentative glance and paused in taking another bite of the food. She turned her head, glancing around at the room. Only the minimal essentials were present. A single bed that was more of a cot, a rolled blanket near the foot of it, a table and two chairs, a small oil cooking stove and pan for washing. The cupboards had no doors and Kella could see just a few jars.

Once again, a strange feeling washed through her. It was not her fault the old woman was too poor to care for herself. She shouldn't care that she was eating the small bit of food the woman offered. If she couldn't afford it, she shouldn't give it away.

Even those thoughts didn't push away the unease she felt as she slowly chewed the bread and cheese. She was hungry. If she was going to be successful on her mission, she needed food. Since she was still weak and in unfamiliar territory, it would be better for someone who knew where to go to retrieve the items she needed.

Satisfied with her reasoning, Kella reached into the small pouch at her waist and pulled out several credits. She slapped them down on the table and shot what she hoped was a fierce glare at the old woman.

"I need food. Here are some credits. Go get more," Kella ordered.

The man cleared his throat and raised an eyebrow at her. Kella returned his look with a defiant one, before it slowly turned to confusion when he didn't back down. She glanced back and forth between Ash and the woman.

"Please," Ash said with a wave of his hand.

Kella's expression cleared. "You are welcome," she replied, picking up another slice of cheese and bread.

Ash released an exasperated sigh. "I think what you *meant* to say is 'Noma, here are some credits. Can you please go to the market for more food?" he suggested.

"That is what I said," Kella mumbled around her mouthful of food.

Kella observed in puzzlement as Ash picked up the credits that she placed on the table and turned to the old woman. He put them in Noma's hand when she reached for them and gave the woman a tender smile. Kella tilted her head when she heard his voice deepen and grow more gentle.

"Noma, would you mind purchasing some more food? It appears we are all hungry and I hate that we are eating you out of house and home," he said.

Noma nodded, her eyes wide with uncertainty. Kella's gaze followed Ash and Noma to the door. Ash opened the door for Noma, making sure he stayed hidden before closing it again after the woman stepped through.

Kella absently chewed the bread and cheese, her gaze following Ash as he returned to the table. He picked up the empty cup and walked over to the counter where a large pitcher sat. He poured more water into the cup before turning and walking back to the table. Her hand instinctively rose for the cup when he held it out. She blinked in surprise when he pulled it just out of her reach.

"Thank you," he said with a raised eyebrow.

"Why should I thank you? I did not ask you to get water for me," Kella said with a frown.

Ash shook his head in resignation and placed the cup on the table in front of her. "No, you didn't, but it is the polite thing to do. Just like you should have asked Noma in a polite tone to purchase more food. You can see that she and Abeni don't have the resources to feed themselves, much less two additional people," he said.

Kella paused in reaching for the cup to frown back at Ash. "It is not the way of the Turbinta," she finally said, picking up the cup and drinking from it.

She froze when Ash's hand covered hers. He was leaning down so they were eye to eye. A surge of warmth swept through her when he slid his fingers down to her wrist and guided the cup to the table before lifting his hand to tenderly brush his thumb over her bruised bottom lip, careful not to touch the cut.

"I'm a human, and it is our way to respect our elders and others. Noma and Abeni's lives have been placed in danger, and an added stress has been incurred by our presence. They were both very gracious to accept us into their home, especially with your injuries," Ash reminded her.

Kella felt her face flush under his soft reproach. "It is not the Turbinta way," she snapped defensively, "...but I will remember your words, human," she continued quietly. She paused a moment, gazing at him. "Is it true? Are you really one of the Ancient Knights of the Gallant?"

Ash brushed the back of his fingers over her cheek before he pulled his hand away. Her body immediately reacted to the loss of his touch. She liked the feel of his warm hand against her skin. It felt... different. The few times Tallei touched Kella, her hands had been cold and impersonal. Some of the patrons of Tallei's bar tried to touch Kella when she was younger, but Tallei had made short work of them. She would not allow anyone to distract Kella from her training or give them a chance to take her away. A Turbinta mentor spent a lot of valuable time and resources training her pupils. They would not tolerate anyone encroaching on their property.

Kella resisted the urge to touch her cheek. Instead, she picked up the last piece of cheese and bread. She warily watched Ash slide into the seat across from her. He leaned forward, both arms resting on the table. Once again, she felt a wave of uncertainty, confusion, and curiosity sweep through her. He did not feel threatened by her.

"No, I'm not some ancient Knight of the Gallant. I'm a Lt. Commander with the United States Navy and a pilot for an international exploration team. I don't know how I ended up here...." He paused and glanced around the room before returning to gaze at her again. A wry smile pulled at his lips. "You have no idea how weird this is to me right now."

"What is weird?" Kella asked in a barely audible voice, mesmerized by the expression on his face.

He chuckled and sat back in his seat. He folded his hands together and raised an amused eyebrow. That was one of the things she noticed about him. There always appeared to be a glint of amusement in his eyes or on his face. She had never seen anyone so happy before.

"That I'm the only one not wearing a Halloween costume," he replied with a deep sigh.

Chapter 10

Ash's sense that he had fallen into some surreal alternate reality was growing by the minute. He really did not have much of a chance to study the woman he rescued earlier. Between the darkness and the Legion soldiers swarming the city like a pack of rats at the dump, his focus had been on finding a safe place to hide until things calmed down a bit.

He was not kidding when he said he felt like the only one not told about the Halloween party. The woman sitting across from him had skin the color of a Douglas Fir tree. Her eyes were the rich color of the bark and her hair was as black as his own, only it looked soft and silky.

He gripped his hands together to keep from reaching across the small table to touch her hair to find out if it felt as soft as it looked. Her face was oval-shaped, and her almond-shaped eyes gave her an exotic look that complemented her coloring. Her nose was slender while her lips were full. Her bottom lip was slightly swollen from her previous fight. She was slender and muscular, far different from his usual taste in women. He normally liked them with a little more meat on their bones, but there was something about Kella that made him want to explore the curves hidden beneath her outfit.

"Why do you look at me in such a way?" she demanded.

Ash couldn't resist giving her his best smile. The one that usually melted the ladies' hearts. The one that always got him – well, almost always – out of trouble. Just to make sure it was effective, he increased the dimple in his left cheek and gave her the smoldering look.

His cheeks were beginning to hurt when he realized that she was still looking at him with that puzzled, what-the-fuck-are-you-doing expression on her face. He tilted his head and changed his expression from smoldering to playful puppy. Her expression didn't change. Ash finally gave up. His cheeks were beginning to get a cramp. He relaxed the muscles in his face and released a sigh.

"You know, most women respond differently. That was my best look," he replied dryly.

She studied him for a moment before she shook her head. "If that is your best, you need more practice. You have very white, flat teeth. Are they real?" she asked.

He raised a hand and slowly ran it down his face. Nope, he never got a reaction like that before. The humor of the situation wasn't lost on him. His grandmother and Josh would be loving this moment if they were here.

Ash decided he must have died and was sent to purgatory for all of his misdeeds when the Gliese 581g went through the gateway. His grandmother warned him it would happen. He should have listened to her. He leaned forward and dejectedly rested his chin on his hand.

"Yes, my teeth are real, and straight thanks to three years of wearing braces when I was a kid," he responded with a rueful sigh.

"Do not feel badly about them. Mine are flat as well. Tallei was going to have them sharpened, but it cost too many credits," she said.

"Who is Tallei?" Ash asked.

Kella hesitated before she shrugged and replied. "She is my mentor," she replied in a quiet voice, rotating the cup of water in her hands.

"Josh's dad and my grandmother were my mentors," Ash said with a nod of understanding. "My grandmother raised me. I never knew my mom. My dad was active military and gone more than he was home. My grandmother was a retired Air Force nurse, so that helped. She was strict."

"Tallei is strict. I nearly died under her hand more than once," Kella said with a hint of pride for her mentor's strength and her own strength derived from those experiences. "It did not happen often of course. I learned not to fail. I became one of the best in training."

Ash's mouth tightened and his eyes flashed with an uncharacteristic anger. "My grandmother didn't believe in using physical violence, especially against kids," he said.

Kella looked at him with a puzzled frown. "But… how could you be trained if you were not beaten? Surely you must have failed, at least once. How could she control you if you did not fear her?" she asked.

"I failed plenty of times. Heck, probably more than I needed to. Grandma felt that failure was just as important as success. If I had succeeded all the time, I wouldn't have learned as much, or become the man I am," Ash explained, reaching across to touch her hand.

Kella started to pull her hand away, but stopped when she realized he wasn't trying to grab her. He turned his hand so that his palm was facing up. He felt an unfamiliar tug in his chest when an expression of uncertainty crossed her face.

She glanced up at his face before looking back down at his hand. He wiggled his fingers and waited. It took a minute before she finally slid her hand into his. He didn't close his fingers around her hand. Something told him that this was all new, unfamiliar territory to Kella and it broke his heart. Instead, he gently caressed her hand as if stroking a small bird.

"My love for my grandmother controlled me. I didn't want to see the disappointment in her eyes when she looked at me. If I tried something and failed, she looked at me with love and compassion and then encouraged me to try again and again until I succeeded. If I did something bad, she would become quiet. She still looked at me with love, but I could see the disappointment, even when she tried to hide it," he murmured in a soft, gentle tone.

Kella stared at him, unblinking. "Tallei does not love. Love is a weak emotion. To love something or someone gives that person power over you and makes you vulnerable. Your enemies will attack that vulnerability. You should not treasure anything, for it will be your downfall," she replied, pulling her hand out of his and clenching her fist.

Ash was about to reply when the door behind them opened. They both rose at the same time. The difference was he wasn't holding a gun aimed at the person who entered.

Ash swore if Abeni could turn any whiter, there wouldn't have been a shred of color on the boy's face. He was holding several bags in his hands and remained frozen on the doorstep. Ash could see Noma behind her grandson. The boy must have found Noma on his return from searching for Hutu.

Deciding he needed to take control of the situation, he stepped around the table and walked toward the door, placing his body between Kella and Abeni. He just hoped Kella did not get a twitch or have to sneeze. If she did, he would be visiting hell a lot more quickly than he wanted to.

"We… have food," Abeni said in a slightly strangled tone that was not completely due to the bruising on it.

"Thank you, Abeni. We're glad you both made it back safely. Aren't we, Kella?" Ash responded with a pointed look over his shoulder.

"Yes, I am still hungry," Kella admitted, lowering her gun and replacing it at her waist. Ash stepped aside so the other two could enter and cleared his throat. Kella flashed him a confused glance before she rolled her eyes in exasperation. She was so cute, Ash had to grin. "Thank you," she added in a stiff voice.

Ash was not sure who looked more startled, Abeni or Noma. It was obvious they were not expecting the polite words from Kella. He followed them back to the table. Abeni placed the bags on the counter before turning to pull two large crates over to the table to make additional seating. Noma quickly unpacked the bags and began preparing them all a more substantial meal.

"Do you need any help, Noma? My grandmother made sure I knew my way around a kitchen," Ash asked.

Noma quickly shook her head. "No, thank you, Ancient Knight. This will not take long," she assured him, peeking over at Kella before turning back to her task.

Ash took up a position on the crate to Kella's left. The position kept him facing the door. Kella recognized what he was doing and moved across to the seat he vacated.

"Were you able to find Hutu and the others?" Ash asked, leaning forward on the table.

Abeni sat down on the other crate and shook his head. Ash couldn't help but think the boy looked very young and tired. He was curious about why Abeni had hooked up with the other man from the alley. *Probably desperation,* he thought as he watched the way the boy kept glancing worriedly at his grandmother.

"No one saw them or has heard of them, at least from what I was able to find out. It is like they vanished," Abeni said.

Ash released a dry laugh and nodded his head. "I imagine Hutu is pretty damn good if he is anything like his father. Do you know who was with him?" he asked, trying to hide the intensity of his need to find out which member might have survived.

"There was a woman and a man. The woman had the markings of a Tesla Terrian. No one saw what the man looked like. He kept his head covered," Abeni replied.

"I saw him," Kella said, glancing at Ash.

"You… How…? Where…? What did he look like?" Ash asked in surprise.

Kella looked uncomfortable for a moment before her face cleared and she shrugged. "It was outside the Sandsabar. He was pale, not a white like Abeni and Noma, more the color of the sand. His hair was a dark brown, almost the color of your skin. He… moved like you did in the alley when you fought those men and spoke words like you do. He also…." Her voice faded and grew troubled.

Ash reached over and picked her right hand up in his. "He also what, Kella?" he asked.

Kella gazed at him with a puzzled expression. "You say you are not one of the Ancient Knights, but if you are like him, then you must be," she murmured.

"Why? Why do you say that?" Ash asked.

Kella studied his face with an intense expression. "Because he carried a staff given to the Knights of the Gallant Order. He fought with it in the way you do. He came from the stars and fell to the planet. It is just like the stories on the disk said," she said in a voice that grew more intense the more she talked.

Ash sensed Abeni and Noma's sudden stillness. He glanced around at the two of them. They were staring at him with a mixture of hope and awe. He swallowed. These people thought he was something he wasn't.

What's important is that Josh is alive, Ash told himself. Sergi's hair was more of a white-blonde the last time he saw him. His accent was also different. It had to be Josh. Once Ash found him, they would figure out their next step together.

Still, he had to at least try to set them straight. Just letting them go on thinking he was…their savior or something – no, he had to say something.

"I know what you are thinking. Kubo said the same thing about the ancients creating a gateway and promising to come back one day when the people of this world needed them again. We did come through a gateway, but it's not what you think," Ash tried to explain, searching their faces.

"Did you fall from the stars?" Kella finally asked.

Ash turned to gaze at Kella. "Yeah. When our spaceship began to break apart, we were forced into the emergency pods on board the Gliese. The pods were ejected into space when the hull was breached. The onboard computer on each pod was programmed to search for the nearest habitable location. My capsule fell to this world. It wasn't like we had much choice, we were dead either way – or so we thought. Those emergency pods were a prototype designed by a bunch of students, but I'll be damned if they didn't work the way they were designed to! We hoped we'd never have to use them because we were sure it would be certain death. None of this would have happened if we hadn't been ordered to see if we could get the gateway working. Sergi was able to fix the damn thing, but the Gliese 581 must have been too close. The gateway activated and sucked us in. The ship couldn't break free of the force without destroying most of the ship. We would never have made it home. Sergi was hurt. Josh refused to leave him. We were able to get them back on board, but it was too late. Josh made the decision to go through it. I don't remember anything after we went through. I woke a few weeks ago out in the desert. I made my way across it, found the road that led to the city, and here I am," Ash said, blinking and pushing the memories away.

"We are glad you are here, Ancient Knight," Noma said, stepping forward and placing two plates filled with food on the table. "You must eat and rest. The city is full of Legion soldiers. It is dangerous for you to journey now. Tomorrow, Abeni and I will learn more and bring you news. We thank you, Turbinta, for your generous credits."

Kella pulled her hand free of Ash's and sat back when Noma returned with another plate of food. Her lips parted at the delicious smells and her stomach growled loudly. She glanced up at Noma with an uncertain look before she nodded her head.

Chapter 11

Several hours later, Ash stepped out of the bathroom. He was surprised when Abeni showed them the room behind a curtained doorway. Ash had thought it was a storage area. He paused and listened to Abeni's soft snores for a moment. The curtains were closed, but he could see Abeni's foot sticking out from under it. Noma and Abeni were good people.

It had taken a bit of convincing, but he and Kella insisted that Noma keep her bed. Abeni slept on a pallet on the floor next to his grandmother. Noma had brought out more blankets and several woven mats for Ash and Kella to make pallets on the floor in the room that made up the kitchen, dining, and living area.

Kella lay on her pallet. His lips twitched and he stopped to stare at her for several long seconds. She was lying on her back with a laser pistol in each hand. The blanket to cover her was still neatly folded next to her. Hell, she hadn't even taken her boots off!

"Do you always sleep like this?" Ash asked, taking off his robe and lowering himself down to his pallet.

Kella turned her head to look at him as he folded the robe next to him. "Yes. It is always better to be prepared," she stated, turning her head to face up again and closing her eyes.

"Prepared for what?" Ash asked, removing his boots.

Kella released a sigh and turned her head to look at him again with a frown. He pulled his legs up and rested his arms on his knees.

"In case someone tries to kill me," Kella finally replied.

Ash raised an eyebrow. "Does that happen often?" he asked in curiosity.

Kella sighed again and rolled onto her side so that she was facing him. "Do you always talk so much and ask so many questions?" she retorted.

Ash chuckled and shook his head. "No. Usually when I'm alone with a beautiful woman, I have better things to do," he teased.

She gazed at him with a curious expression. "Like what?" she asked.

Ash glanced at the pistols in her hands. "You put those pistols away and I might show you," he said.

Her eyes narrowed and her lips tightened. Ash didn't know why he felt like teasing her. There was just something about her that goaded him to break through the icy reserve she wore like a shield of protection around her.

"If you try to harm me, I will slit your throat," she warned, slowly placing both pistols on her other side.

Ash's eyes twinkled with mischief. What was it about this woman threatening to kill him that turned him on? He didn't think his long abstinence was the reason. She was exotic, curious, yet cautious, and had an air of innocence that he had always avoided in women as if it were the plague. His mind was telling him to stop, that he was treading on dangerous ground while his body was doing a damn football chant!

"Honey, the last thing on my mind is trying to harm you," he promised, the bad boy side of him slamming the door on rational thought. "I have just one more question."

She suspiciously eyed him. "What?"

"Are you sure you are ready for this?" Ash asked, twisting around so he could close the distance between them.

He saw her swallow. Her eyes widened and a trace of hesitancy flickered through them before she blinked it away. He really liked the way she lifted her chin in defiance. It was like waving a red flag in front of a bull and taunting him to do something about it.

Ash crawled the short distance, pacing it to build the anticipation. This was going to be a true test of wills. Hers to keep from killing him and his to keep from taking it beyond the teasing. Right now, his body was clamoring to ignore the danger – and the fact that they weren't exactly alone – and take care of his physical desires. Josh had always warned him that he better be careful of playing with fire. His friend always swore that one day Ash would meet his match and find a lady who was too hot to handle.

"What… what are you doing?" Kella asked, rolling over onto her back when Ash leaned over her.

Ash gazed down into Kella's eyes. He lifted his left hand and tenderly ran the tips of his fingers along her silky hair. It was coarser than he'd thought it would be, but still soft to the touch. He continued his exploration, running his fingers along the curve of her cheek. His eyes darkened with emotion when he saw the bruising on it. Unable to resist, he bent and brushed a kiss against the discolored flesh. He made sure he didn't press against the damaged tissue.

"I should have killed the men like you said," Ash murmured against her skin.

"Ye… yes… you… should have. Leaving… leaving them alive… leaving them alive…. Ash…."

Kella's hesitant, disjointed words told him that she wasn't any more immune to him than he was to her. It would appear that nature, and their pheromones, were in sync. Whatever in the hell was going on, he liked it.

"I want to kiss you, but I don't want to hurt you," Ash groaned in frustration.

Kella turned her head. The move placed her lips almost directly under his. He could feel her warm breath against his lips.

"How would you hurt me?" she asked.

"You have a busted and bruised lip. The way I want to kiss you – well, let's just say gentle isn't part of what I want to be at the moment," he replied.

She touched her bottom lip where it was bruised with the tip of her tongue. Ash bit back the muttered curse he wanted to release. She was not making this any easier on him. The bad part was: he suspected she wasn't even aware of that fact.

"It doesn't hurt," she whispered.

"You probably shouldn't have told me that, Kella," Ash moaned.

He lowered his head and captured her lips in a heated but tender kiss. Her lips parted in a gasp and he took advantage of it, running his tongue along her smooth teeth before tangling with her tongue. In that moment, Ash knew he was in big trouble.

..*

Kella didn't know what to expect, but this was not it. She had seen men and women together before; it would have been difficult to work in Tallei's bar and not see those who came to relieve their needs, but confusion swept through her at the magnitude of emotions stirring inside her. How could the touching of lips cause so much reaction?

She lifted her hands to his chest. Her intention had been to push him away. That thought faded when he touched his tongue to hers and her hands encountered a warm, hard, muscular chest hidden under the soft, thin shirt. Tallei had always warned Kella that her curiosity would get her into trouble. Kella pushed the thought of her mentor away. Tallei was not here and Kella didn't want to stop. She wanted to explore these new feelings raging inside of her.

Her hands slid up his chest and along his shoulders. Her fingers touched the skin at the back of his neck, enjoying the warmth radiating from him. There had been so many nights when she shivered in the cold. Tallei had told her it was to condition her. Tallei had told her many, many things over the years.

But, Tallei isn't here now, she vaguely thought, pulling Ash closer to her.

..*

Ash pulled hard on the reins of his emotions. Warning bells were blaring inside of him. He swept his hand down along Kella's side, bracing most of his weight on his right hand. Her slight wince reminded him of the blows she received to her side and helped him regain a small fraction of his self-control.

It was several minutes later before he reluctantly released her lips. They were swollen and glistening. He closed his eyes and willed his body to listen to him.

"Damn girl, you are hot," Ash murmured before he opened his eyes and pushed back up onto his haunches.

Kella blinked up at him, her eyes dazed and unfocused. "I am not hot. It is very cool in here," she replied.

Ash chuckled and shook his head. He glanced over toward the curtained alcove when he heard Abeni release a series of short snores. Nothing like a chaperone and a bruised heroine to keep the hero in line, not that he thought of himself as much of a hero.

With a grunt, Ash pushed up and out of Kella's reach. He turned and gathered his pallet, robe, and blankets. He left his boots where he placed them.

"Where are you going?" Kella asked, sitting up to stare at him.

Ash rolled his shoulders and drew in a deep breath to calm his body and mind before he turned to look at her. He dragged the pallet closer to hers and lined it up. If he was going to apply for superhero status, he might as well go all the way.

"Well, I can't have you catching a cold after saving your life, now can I? We have a long day ahead of us tomorrow and you need to get some rest so your body can heal. I don't know about you, but I hate being cold when I'm trying to get a good night's sleep," Ash stated

"What are you doing?" Kella asked in confusion when he reached down and took the blanket she had set to the side.

Ash shook out the blanket and sat down on his pallet. He used both of the blankets to cover them up before he laid back and motioned for her to lean up a little bit. She hesitated a moment before she did. He slid his arm under her head to act as a pillow and pulled her against his body.

"I'm going to keep you warm," he said, turning his head and brushing a kiss against her temple.

"Oh." She paused for a moment. "Ash?"

"Yes, Kella."

She turned slightly into him. "Will you tell me more about this Josh and the woman who raised you with love?" she asked in a quiet voice.

A small smile curved Ash's lips. He stared up at the ceiling and thought about some of the more humorous adventures he and Josh had growing up. It was amazing that neither of them were ever seriously injured or killed.

"Lesson number 432 according to my grandma, never let two teenage boys near a biplane unsupervised. When Josh and I were sixteen, we took a Stearman Biplane for a joyride. We just watched the Great Waldo Pepper and decided we could do a better job of wing walking…," Ash chuckled as he reminisced about that adventure.

He spoke in a low, calm tone, losing himself in the story. Josh always told him that he had a gift for the tales. He might have embellished a little, but most of it was true. It wasn't until he started his third story that he felt Kella's body relax and knew she was finally falling asleep. He continued talking until he felt her soft sigh and heard her even breathing – only then did his voice fade.

Ash lay on the hard floor deep in thought. He had come to terms with the fact that he would probably never see Earth again before the Gliese had departed. It hadn't been an easy decision, but he knew he was giving up his life for a greater cause. He had no one left back on Earth to tie him down. His friendship with Josh was the only thing that he had of value.

He hadn't liked the idea of being celibate for the rest of his life, but staying alive and keeping a spaceship together was a full-time, exhausting job. Now, he needed to come to terms with a new life in a world that was decidedly foreign. These were new cultures, new environments, new everything.

"Josh, I sure could use some of your calm logic right about now, man. I sure hope you and the others made it," Ash whispered before releasing a sigh and closing his eyes.

He focused on relaxing his body. Fortunately, sleep didn't take long to come after the busy day he had. It also didn't take long for his tired mind to fill with vivid dreams of spaceships and alien worlds; or, for the image of a beautiful, exotic, green-skinned woman to make him want the dreams to come true.

Chapter 12

"Wake," Abeni's low, urgent voice whispered.

Ash's eyes opened and he nodded. He was fortunate he was one of those who woke alert. It had been a necessity both in his career in the Navy and on the Gliese. He turned his head and noticed the pallet next to him was empty. Hell, he must have been more tired than he thought for everyone but him to be already moving. Rolling to his feet, he ran a hand over his hair and down his face before dropping it.

Noma was quietly collecting items and putting them into a bag. Kella was coming out of the bathroom, and Abeni moved to roll up his pallet. Abeni murmured something to Noma in the Torrian language. Ash only caught the word hurry.

"What is it?" Ash asked.

"The Legion forces are searching each home," Abeni replied.

"Director Andronikos' forces have no authority here, but he ignores that," Noma replied.

Ash watched Noma smooth a withered hand over her hair. Regret filled him that he had brought trouble to her home. It would be better if he disappeared into the city and find Kubo again. He could seek refuge with him. It would only be a matter of time before Kubo was able to contact Hutu and he could find out if Josh was the stranger. Hell, with the way his luck was going, Hutu might be in the underground city enjoying some family time with Kubo and Natta and his other thirty-eight imaginary siblings!

"How long before they get here?" Ash asked.

He grabbed his boots, sat down on one of the crates by the table, and slid them on. His gaze flickered over to Kella. She had been decidedly quiet in the few minutes since he awakened. Her gaze flashed to him before she quickly looked away. In that brief moment, he saw the confusion in her eyes once again. He would love to reassure her that she wasn't the only one confused. Last night was a first for him. He never slept with a woman in his arms that he hadn't made love to first.

"Not long; I saw soldiers three streets over," Abeni stated.

Ash absently nodded. He rose from the crate and started to reach for the protective robe when Kella bent and picked it up. His hand reached for it when she held it out to him. Once again, she had that calm mask on her face.

"Your lip isn't as swollen," he murmured, lifting a hand to touch it.

She stepped back and nodded. "I heal quickly. It is one of the reasons Tallei chose me," she said, turning away from him to pick up her bedding.

Ash pulled his robe on and fastened it. He picked up his head scarf and wrapped it in the fashion of the Torrians and adjusted the lower section over his face before sliding on the goggles.

"I think it is best if I return to a friend of mine here. The more distance I place between you and

Noma, the safer you will be," Ash stated, picking up the rifle and sliding it over his shoulder.

"You know others here?" Kella asked in surprise, turning to look at him again.

Ash grinned at her worried expression. She could see the amusement her concern brought to him. His gaze swept over her face. She was right. She did heal fast. The bruise on her cheek was barely visible.

"I met someone. He's a crazy old man, but he knows his way around. What will you do?" Ash asked.

She raised her eyebrow at him. "Go with you," she stated in a cool tone.

"Go with…. I don't think that's such a good idea, Kella. In case you haven't noticed, the Legion is crawling all over the place looking for someone. I hate to admit it, but I could be that person," Ash replied with a shake of his head. "As much as I'd love to spend more time with you, darling, I don't think it would be wise for you to be seen with me."

Kella stepped closer to him and lifted her chin. The smile that faded from his lips returned. Damn, but he loved that stubborn tilt to her chin. It was sexy as hell.

"My name is not darling, it is Kella. Remember that. I go where you go. That is also not going to change," she bit out in a hard tone.

"I apologize for interrupting your argument, but it is best if you leave before the soldiers arrive," Abeni interrupted.

Ash glanced at the boy's nervous face. Abeni was right; he and Kella didn't have the time to argue at the moment. Ash nodded and turned toward the doorway. Abeni hurried forward. He cracked it open to peer outside. His loud hiss and softly muttered curse drew all of their attention.

"What is it?" Ash asked, walking over to stand behind the boy so he could see outside.

Across from them were four Legion soldiers – and the man from the alley who had been with Abeni last night. The man was talking to the soldiers, pointing to his head, and then waving his hands in moves reminiscent of the ones Ash used when he was fighting him last night. Abeni closed the door when the soldiers turned in their direction.

"What will we do? Carbo will kill me," Abeni said in a trembling voice. His eyes were wide with fear. "The Legion… I have heard what they do to their prisoners. Noma…."

Ash glanced around the tiny room. "Is there another way out of here?" he asked.

"No," Noma replied.

Ash watched her place the bag on the table in resignation. His lips tightened into a grim line. He wasn't quitting just yet. He would give himself up before he allowed Noma, Abeni, or Kella to be harmed because of his presence.

"What is behind the relief room wall?" Kella asked with a nod in the direction of the bathroom.

Abeni stared at Kella in confusion. "The back alley," he replied.

Kella turned to gaze at Ash. "You block the door so no one can enter, I will make a door to the alley. You two will have to come with us. Abeni was right. The Legion will use your love for each other against you to gain information," she instructed with a pointed look at Ash.

"How will you make a door through these walls? They have to be at almost a meter thick," Ash asked.

"I have my ways. You must be prepared to exit quickly. Do not breathe in the gas. It will quickly overcome you," Kella said, turning toward the bathroom. "Let me know when you are ready. We will not have long to exit the dwelling."

Ash didn't ask any more questions. He and Abeni picked up the crates and placed them in front of the door before moving the table and bracing it at an angle to jam it. Noma stood to the side of the kitchen counter and the opening of the bathroom while Kella stood in the doorway.

Kella had ripped the curtain down and torn several pieces from it. She held one out to Noma and another to Abeni. From her waist, she pulled a small cup-shaped object and held it over her nose and mouth. With the push of a button, it expanded, creating a filtered mask.

"Ready," Ash said before drawing in a deep breath and holding it.

Kella nodded and turned. With a flick of her wrist, she threw something toward the back wall. Ash barely caught a glimpse of the small, silver and black device before it disappeared. Almost immediately, smoke rolled out from the room.

He watched Kella turn and grip Noma's arm. With a wave of his hand, he motioned for Abeni to follow the two women. He shouldered the rifle and stepped through the dense smoke, glad he was wearing the goggles. At the same time, a loud thump on the door and a booming voice ordered them to open up.

..*

Kella stepped over the crumbled remains of the mud-bricks and into the back alley. She glanced both ways before turning to help Noma through. The old woman drew in a gasping breath. Her eyes glistened with tears from the smoke. Abeni stepped through next. He was trying not to cough.

"Ash…," she started to say, concerned before she saw him appear through the smoke.

"We have to go that way, the other way is a dead end," Abeni choked out.

The small group moved down the narrow alley. Kella felt uneasy. There were a dozen or so doors on either side of the alley. She eyed them warily as they passed. The alley was a death trap – narrow, long, and with limited exits.

She breathed a sigh of relief when they reached the end of it. Peering around the corner to see if the coast was clear, she leaned back and gazed at Ash. He stepped around Noma and Abeni to stand next to her.

"Where is your friend?" Kella asked.

Ash glanced around the corner, trying to get his bearings. It was dark last night when they arrived, and he and Abeni wove through the streets to avoid the soldiers. A frown of frustration creased his brow and he shook his head.

"If we can get back to the Sandsabar, I can guide us from there," he said.

"Abeni will have to guide us. I am not familiar with the city enough to know its location either," Kella admitted, glancing around Ash to the boy. "You can lead us back to the Sandsabar?"

"Yes," Abeni responded.

"We'll follow you," Ash replied.

Kella glanced around the corner again, scanning it. She waited until a large group of pedestrians walked by before they merged in with them. Abeni kept a slow, steady pace. He glanced back over his shoulder frequently to make sure he wasn't going too fast for his grandmother.

Frustration burned through Kella. Tallei always told her that the Turbinta moved like shadows, even during the day. They did not walk in the sun where they could be seen. She focused on her skin coloring, changing it from her natural green to the red of the Torrians. Her ability to become a chameleon allowed her to walk where most assassins couldn't – among their targets.

Kella glance back at Ash. He was scanning the crowds as well, searching for danger. She turned away before he sensed her appraisal. What was it about him that confused her? He was her target, she was sure of that, so why did she hesitate?

She could have eliminated Abeni and Noma last night and incapacitated Ash while he slept, then notified the Legion Director that she had captured one of the creatures from the fallen capsules. True, she had no proof except the story Ash told her and his odd physical and verbal characteristics, but she could have left it to Andronikos to prove who Ash was. She was hired to find and deliver, not to verify his history.

Yet, she was unable to bring herself to harm the boy and old woman – and Ash. She thought of the stories he told her last night. Love – Ash said love controlled him, and yet, so far it had not led to a short life. He had described how it made him stronger, not weaker. He held her close to his body to keep her warm and shared his blanket; and while he kissed her, he did not try anything else, which confused her even more.

Kella wanted to growl in frustration. This was her first mission and all she found was confusion, uncertainty, and a man who made her feel things she had thought she was immune to. She was also quickly running out of time. The Director gave her until the end of the lunar cycle. Her time was already half elapsed.

"Stop!" a shout from behind them rang through the crowded street.

Kella turned to look over her shoulder. Her hands automatically moved to the two laser pistols at her sides. Six Legion soldiers, two more than before, were pushing through the crowd toward them. In front of the group was another man who looked like he was beaten badly from the gash across his forehead and the bruising down one side of his face.

"Carbo!" Abeni hissed.

"Get your grandmother out of here," Kella instructed, aiming her gun at the man in front. He was unprotected and a liability. If Ash had killed the man instead of beating him up, the soldiers would never have found them. She squeezed the trigger, and a dark hole appeared in the center of the informant's forehead. His body froze for half a second as if it took a moment for it to realize what happened before collapsing. The suddenness of it caused two of the soldiers to stumble over the body in front of them. Kella took out the two soldiers before they could recover.

"Shit!" Ash cursed in a loud voice. "There are civilians!"

"They will help provide protection," Kella retorted.

She fired at the other four soldiers who were trying to seek shelter. Ash lifted the rifle and fired. Another soldier twisted and fell. The other three split up. One took the right side of the street while the other two took the left side. Pedestrians ran in all directions looking for a way to escape.

Kella yelled for Ash to follow her. They both turned and began threading their way as quickly as possible through the panicked crowds. It didn't take them long to catch up with Noma and Abeni. Noma was struggling to move through the throng of people.

"You must go on without me," Noma replied in a tired voice.

"Like hell," Ash said.

Kella realized he meant it – he would not leave the old woman behind even if it endangered them all. Kella glanced around. An empty push cart sat near an abandoned stall.

"The cart, put her in it," Kella ordered. "Abeni can push her. You go ahead. I will take care of the guards."

Ash's hand shot out and gripped her upper arm. It was impossible to see the look in his eyes or the expression on his face due to the goggles and covering, but she could feel the steel in his grip. She shook her head.

"I will catch up with you, Ash. I promise," Kella said.

His fingers tightened for a moment before they relaxed. His hand dropped back to his side and he turned away. Kella paused for a brief moment, observing as Abeni helped Noma into the cart, hurried around to pick up the handles, and began to push her down a side alley at a brisk pace.

Turning her attention back to the soldiers cautiously making their way down the street, she stepped behind a market stall and waited. They would have called for reinforcements. She would need to make sure she took these soldiers out before the reinforcements arrived. As she expected, they moved back into formation once they believed the threat was gone.

Kella waited until they were in the center of the street before she stepped out and started firing. The first two dropped quickly. She went into a roll and came up in a crouch, shooting a series of blasts when a third soldier returned fire. She winced when one of his blasts grazed her shoulder. Only when he finally dropped to the ground and remained motionless did she turn back toward the alley. Now, she needed to catch up with Ash and the others.

Behind her, street merchants and pedestrians returned to their daily activities as if nothing had happened. Kella didn't see the group of men who appeared like ghosts to remove the bodies – or the old blind man who stood in the shadows. When the reinforcements did arrive, they did not see anything amiss.

Chapter 13

Ash, Abeni, and Noma emerged out of another back alley and into the crowds. This street was calmer than many of the others. Ash started to recognize some of the buildings and realized they were just a few blocks from the Sandsabar.

Kella hadn't joined them yet. Ash had to continually fight the urge to turn around and look to see if she was behind them. He hadn't missed the fear people exuded when they saw her. Hell, he would have given her a wide berth too if he'd seen someone coming at him packing the heat she was wearing.

Ash knew Kella could take care of herself. It was just a few guards – a significant threat to the two he was protecting, but not to her if her moves earlier were any indication of her abilities to protect herself. She would come join them soon. They needed to keep moving.

The cart was awkward with so many people. Ash was glad to be free of it for a bit after he parked it in the shade along the side of the road and told Abeni and Noma what he was going to do. He was going back for Kella.

As he backtracked, he spotted Legion soldiers in the midst of the crowd, but Ash knew if he kept his head down, he'd be fine. He was one in a sea of people all dressed pretty much the same.

He was replaying in his mind how her skin had been the familiar forest green one minute, and Torrian red the next. It was enough to blow his mind. He was trying to process how she did it when he ran into a group of Legion soldiers as soon as he turned the corner of the alley.

Lost in thought, he made the mistake of mumbling a curse word when a Legion soldier pushed him back against a table filled with merchandise. Irritation filled him for a brief moment, but the soldier wasn't even looking at him, he was just trying to bully his way through the crowd.

"Damn, take a chill pill, dude," Ash muttered under his breath.

The soldier froze and his gaze zeroed in on the man who had spoken with an unfamiliar accent in the universal language.

Shit.

"Drop your weapon and remove your face coverings," the soldier ordered.

"Okay, okay, keep your pantyhose on," Ash muttered.

The soldier had eight of his buddies nearby. Ash noticed them in all. If there had been half that many, he wouldn't have thought twice about kicking their asses. If the number wasn't intimidating enough, each of the eight held a lethal looking weapon aimed at his head and chest.

Ash held his left hand out while he shrugged the rifle off of his right shoulder. Holding it out, he dropped it to the ground. Next, he slowly reached up and pulled off the goggles. An unexpected sense of déjà vu swept through him.

"Hey, guys, how's it hanging?" Ash asked.

The soldier speaking to him looked at him in surprise. Ash gave the soldier a cocky grin right before he threw his goggles. This probably wasn't going to end well, but he wasn't going down without a fight.

The man's instinctive response was what he was hoping for. When the tip of the man's rifle rose up in the air, Ash grabbed the end of it, forcing the soldier off balance while doing a high kick to the chin of the man standing next to him. He pulled on the end of the rifle, jerking the soldier toward him, then swung the man around and slung him against the four men standing behind him. His elbow struck out at the soldier on his left. Two more soldiers started toward him before falling face first onto the street, dark burn marks scorched into the back of their uniforms.

Ash barely had time to jerked back when one of the soldiers shot at him. The man's aim went slightly wide thanks to the long walking stick that knocked the rifle upward at the last moment. Ash ducked when the long walking stick swung around toward his head. The loud crack told him that there had been a Legion soldier coming up behind him.

In a matter of seconds, the eight guards were either unconscious or dead. The crowd, which paused to watch what was happening, quickly dispersed when Kubo slammed his walking stick into the ground. Ash turned in time to watch Kella striding toward him with a furious expression on her face.

"You… You could have been killed," Kella snarled in a furious tone.

"But, I wasn't," he replied.

He stumbled back a step when she aimed one of her pistols at him. He held up his hands, a surprised grin curved his lips, and he shrugged nonchalantly. Obviously his lack of remorse was not helping her temper because her eyes flashed and she actually growled at him.

"It is not amusing," she snapped, stopping in front of him and glaring at him with disapproval.

Ash's gaze softened. "Did you know you are beautiful when you are angry?" he asked.

Kella snapped her teeth at him and turned to aim her pistol at one of the soldiers when the man groaned. Ash grabbed her wrist to stop her from shooting him at the same time that Kubo popped the guy on the head, effectively silencing him. Ash shook his head. He was going to have to remember that aliens were as bloodthirsty as humans.

"I suggest we get out of here before they wake up or more arrive," Ash stated, turning to Kubo. "Thanks, old man."

Kubo chuckled. "I am not as old as you think, Ashton Haze."

"… or as blind. I swear you are pulling my leg, Kubo," Ash muttered.

"There are many levels of blindness – not all are with the eyes," Kubo retorted. "Let us retreat from the eyes of the Legion forces."

Ash turned to Kella when he felt her tremble. It was only then that he realized he was still holding onto her wrist. He glanced at her just in time to see her gaze skitter away from him. Ash looked over at Abeni and Noma where they waited in the shadows, expressions of uncertainty and apprehension on their faces.

"Kubo, I have two others who need your protection," Ash said.

Kubo turned his head in the direction of Abeni and Noma. One of Kubo's men murmured to him. Kubo replied in a low voice.

"My men will see that they are taken to a safe place," Kubo replied. "What of the Turbinta?"

"Kella? She's with me. At least…." Ash started to say, turning to look down at Kella.

"I am with Ash," Kella confirmed in a tone that brooked no argument.

Kubo's lips twitched. "I hope you realize what you are doing, Ashton Haze. Let us return to the safety of the caverns. My men will take care of the soldiers," Kubo said.

Ash grunted and released Kella's hand. He wasn't sure exactly when his grip on her wrist had loosened and slid down until his hand was holding hers. Amusement, and some other emotion he couldn't quite put his finger on, caught him off-guard.

He didn't need to try to catch her gaze to know that she wouldn't look him in the eye right at that moment. There was something about her brash strength and surprising shyness that fascinated him. The combination of alpha toughness and vulnerability was sure to make for an intriguing relationship. All he had to do was convince Kella that they could make a dynamic team if she gave him a chance.

Ash bent and retrieved the rifle he dropped, along with his goggles. Then he and Kella followed Kubo. A quick glance told him that Abeni and Noma were already gone. A swift shaft of regret swept through him. He didn't have the chance to thank them for their help and apologize for endangering their lives. He would have to make sure that Kubo understood how much he owed the boy and his grandmother. He didn't know how he would pay the old man back, but he would find a way.

..*

"I have ordered a search of every building, General Landais," Commander Shec Jatur said.

"What of the many spacecraft leaving the planet?" Roan Landais asked.

"I have ordered each ship searched as well, but there are thousands of them. Without additional troops, it will be impossible to search them all. This is a major spaceport with hundreds of flights arriving and departing daily. There are also many landing areas outside the city," Commander Jatur replied.

Sweat beaded on Shec's upper lip. He resisted the urge to wipe it away and hoped General Landais couldn't see it on the video display. He swallowed when he saw his commanding officer's eyes flash in irritation.

"I do not want excuses, Commander Jatur. I want Hutu Gomerant and those who were with him. Is that clear?" General Landais instructed.

"Yes… Yes, General," Shec replied.

"Contact me when you have relevant information," General Landais ordered before ending the call.

Shec sat back in his chair. He was aboard one of the smaller command ships which were equipped for planetary use. He glanced up when the door to his makeshift office chimed.

"Enter," he ordered, lifting a hand to wipe the nervous sweat off of his upper lip.

The door opened and one of his ground patrol leaders stepped inside and walked forward to stand at attention in front of the desk. The man kept his gaze forward, staring over Shec's head. Shec scanned the man's dirty uniform, noting the blood on his temple and the discoloration on his cheek where a bruise had formed.

"What happened?" Shec demanded.

The soldier turned his gaze to meet Shec's intense stare. "We were responding to a call from Squadron Six. A civilian alerted them to a possible sighting. An investigation of the dwelling showed the residents broke through a back wall and escaped. The suspects were intercepted several blocks later," the soldier stated before his voice faded and he pressed his lips together.

"Well… Was it General Gomerant?" Shec demanded, pushing his chair back and rising out of his seat.

The soldier shook his head. "No, sir. Squadron Six and the civilian have disappeared. My squadron…. we were on our way to back up Squadron Six when a civilian bumped into me. He was dressed as a Torrian local, but there was something different about the way he spoke. I instructed him to remove his head covering and goggles. He… was of a species I have not seen before," the soldier said.

"What did he look like?" Shec demanded.

"His skin was a dark brown, as were his eyes. There was not much visible. He overpowered the seven soldiers and myself using fighting skills I have never seen before. Two men were killed," the soldier replied.

Shec's eyebrows rose. "He killed two soldiers and defeated six more by himself?" he demanded in disbelief.

The soldier shook his head. "He had help. I saw… I believe I saw a Turbinta assassin and a blind man before I lost consciousness. When I woke, I was several miles outside the city. I…. The rest of the squadron is still missing," he replied in a quiet tone.

Shec watched the soldier lean forward and place a disk on the desk in front of him. He frowned and bent to pick it up. He turned it over, but there were no markings on it.

"What is this?" Shec demanded, returning his gaze to the soldier's face.

"It was with me when I woke. I did not have it before. I have not looked at the information," the soldier stated.

Shec's fist closed around the disk. So, the resistance was now using Legion soldiers as a messenger. Shec's lips tightened in annoyance.

"Dismissed," Shec ordered.

"Yes, sir," the soldier replied, taking several steps back before he turned sharply on his heel and exited the room.

Shec sank back down onto his chair. His hand trembled slightly as he inserted the disk into the computer in front of him. He sat back, stunned when an image of a large, rectangular object appeared in front of him.

"The Ancient Knights have returned and the new Order of the Knights of the Gallant have risen. The first awakening of the resistance has begun and the time of the Legion rule is coming to an end," a voice stated calmly before the image faded.

This time, sweat beaded on Shec's brow and ran down the collar of his uniform. He played the message several times, pausing to stare at the scorched image painted on the side of the capsule. It was identical to the one on the patch found at a farm outside of town. He pulled out a cloth and wiped his face before he touched the communications panel.

"General Landais, I have a message you should see. I'm uploading it now," Shec said.

Chapter 14

"Are you still not talking to me?" Ash asked, leaning back against the wall and watching Kella sharpen her knives.

She continued to ignore him. An amused smile curved his lips. For the past two days, she had given him the silent treatment. She had stomped, huffed, puffed, and blown him off. He could see the fury still burning in her eyes, but every once in a while, when she thought he wasn't looking, he also caught a look of confusion.

"You know, I don't think I've ever met, much less dated, a woman with that many weapons on her before," he said casually, tilting his head to look at the impressive display. "I'm honestly surprised you can even stand up. They must weigh a ton."

Kella paused, her shoulders stiff with anger before she shook her head and picked up the largest blade and turned to face him. Ash eyed her warily when she bounced it in her hand before she stepped closer to him. He straightened his leg, placing his foot on the ground instead of having it up on the carved stone bench where he was sitting.

She turned the blade in her hand so the handle was facing him and held it out. He ran a hand down his pants before he reached for it. He blinked in surprise at how light the knife was, especially considering the amount of metal in the blade.

"It is important not to be slowed down. The Turbinta use a special metal to form weapons. It is strong, yet light. A good Turbinta mentor instructs their pupils how to create a weapon that is made for them alone. The handle is custom-made for my grip. The balance is designed for my style of fighting," she explained.

"Interesting," Ash said.

He stood up and stepped away from her to an area in the large common room clear of any obstacles. Holding the knife in his right hand, he began doing the Naname-tsuki kata. The moves when done in slow motion were mesmerizing. He executed each graceful move with a natural instinct born from years of training. When he was finished, he turned toward Kella and bowed, holding out the knife she had given him.

"What did you just do? I have never seen anything so beautiful before," Kella asked in a quiet voice.

"Judo," Ash replied with a smile. "It is a form of self-defense."

Kella looked at him with a skeptical expression. "How can a dance keep you safe?" she asked.

Ash chuckled. "Come at me with the knife," he instructed.

"No," she said, starting to turn away.

"Come on. It will be alright," Ash assured her.

Kella shook her head and glanced at him before staring out the doorway. He could see the doubt in her eyes. At least it was better than the anger, and she was talking to him again, so he was making progress.

"Ash, it is not safe for me to come at you with a weapon," Kella finally said, turning to look at him.

"I won't hurt you. I promise," he replied with that crooked smile that showed off his dimple.

***

Kella released an exasperated sigh. This strange man was driving her crazy! For the last two days, he had teased and tried to provoke her into talking to him. His behavior had greatly undermined her determination to remain mad at him for the stunt he pulled back at the market. No one in their right mind would take on eight Legion soldiers alone – in broad daylight.

When she finally made it to the alley and saw him surrounded, she had planned to sneak up on the soldiers. She made it halfway to them when Ash suddenly began doing his strange moves. Granted, he had been doing well on his own, but there was no way he could have succeeded alone in taking down all those men. She shot two of the soldiers when they lifted their weapons to fire on him. An uncharacteristic fear had filled her along with a fury she never felt before.

She turned the knife in her hand. Perhaps if she showed him how dangerous it was here, or on any world, he would be more careful. She didn't question why she should care; she just knew he had to understand that this was different from what his grandmother had taught him. The world was not a good place. It was a dark and dangerous one.

Gripping the knife in her hand, she turned and moved as if to attack him. Her breath hissed out when a second later, she found herself leaning forward in an awkward position and the blade in her hand was deftly removed from her numb fingers. She slowly straightened when Ash released her arm and pulled her against his body.

"The first lesson I learned: don't let anger blind or guide you. Find your center, your balance, and open yourself to everything that is going on around you," Ash murmured in her ear.

Kella struck at him again. Her elbow caught him a glancing blow. When she tried to wrap her foot around his ankle to pull him off balance, she felt her body lifted off the ground. Ash caught her in his arms before she hit the hard surface of the floor. She stared up at him in shock.

"Next I learned to anticipate my opponent's moves by recognizing how he or she uses the muscles in their body," he said, pulling her back to her feet.

"I learned the same," she replied.

She lifted her knee, aiming for his groin, but he blocked her. Fascinated, she struck out again and again, using the moves Tallei taught her. Ash blocked her most of the time. She landed a few good blows, but she was more curious about processing his techniques. Sometimes, he surprised her, capturing her and holding her in a way that made it impossible for her to move, while at other times flipping her so quickly, she was looking up at the ceiling before she knew what had happened.

She rolled and pushed up off the floor. Her eyes glittered with determination when she saw the mischievous grin on Ash's face. She wiped her hands down her black trousers and cracked her neck. Keeping her gaze on him, she twisted enough to pick up two blades from the table.

"This is one of the few times I genuinely miss my vision. Ash, you might need this," Kubo said, his voice laced with amusement.

Ash raised his hand and caught the long walking stick that Kubo used to help guide him. She watched warily as Ash twirled it. The movements were precise, fluid, and unusual. Curious, she lashed out at him. He deflected her attack with a sharp stinging slam.

They circled each other. Once again, he blocked each of her attacks. His use of the long walking stick was reminiscent of the other man using the Staff of the Gallant Order. Before she realized what happened, both of her blades went sliding across the floor and she found herself pinned against Ash's body with the long walking stick pressed against her throat.

"Release me," she ordered, her hands clutching the stick to keep it from cutting off her air supply.

A shiver went through her when she felt his warm breath against her cheek. His lips touched the curve of her earlobe. Tilting her head to the side, she drew in a deep breath.

"For a price," Ash replied.

Kella felt her body tense. "Price? What is your price?" she asked warily.

"Nothing too dire. A kiss would be nice, but I'll settle for a truce if a kiss is too high a price," Ash chuckled.

Kella's lips twitched in amusement. They had attracted a rather large audience. She would demand a price of her own. She nodded in agreement, unwrapping her fingers from the stick and holding her hands up to show she would not fight.

She turned when Ash swung the walking stick away from her throat and tossed it in the direction of Kubo's guard. The old man reached out his hand and grabbed it before his guard could. An inelegant snort escaped her. Ash was right; the old man must be tricking them about his vision impairment because Kubo saw far more than most.

"So, what will it be? A kiss or a truce?" Ash asked.

"I want you to teach me how to fight like you do. You are good, even if I did go easy on you," she retorted with a mischievous grin, not answering his question.

Ash raised an eyebrow. She could see the doubt reflected in his eyes. Curious, she slid her hands up his chest to his shoulders.

"That wasn't part of the deal," he pointed out.

Kella rose up until her lips were a breath away from his. "Please," she whispered, gazing into his eyes.

His eyes widened. "Damn, woman, but you make it hard to resist. Yes," he said.

Kella grinned. It felt odd and unfamiliar. She couldn't remember the last time she smiled – in fact, she wasn't sure she had ever smiled before. A sense of freedom and a curious sense of playfulness flooded her. Leaning forward, she pressed her lips to his before quickly stepping back in excitement.

"Now? You will teach me now?" she asked.

"You are…." Ash started to say before he paused and drew in a deep breath. "Yes, we'll have our first lesson now."

..*

Several hours later, Ash groaned and sank down next to Kubo. He couldn't resist releasing another moan just for good measure when his muscles protested. He sat back, closed his eyes, and ignored the old man's soft chuckle.

"You know, it is probably not wise to teach a Turbinta how to fight like you do. There is always the chance that the master may one day be defeated by the pupil," Kubo said.

"Tell me about it. Kella is a fast learner," Ash retorted, wincing when he pressed against his ribs. "I think I have a bruise."

Kubo's loud laughter echoed through the room. Several people paused and smiled at them before resuming what they were doing. Ash gazed around the area and sighed. A group of men and women chatted while they cleared the remains of the dinner. The enormous hall was used for both dining and socializing. Four sections of long tables sat in the center of the room with benches and chairs placed around them for after dinner talks. It would appear the Torrians were a very social species.

"Greetings, Aston Haze," Natta greeted.

Ash grinned up at Natta. "Hi Natta. I was wondering where you were. I haven't seen you around the last few days," he replied, gingerly sitting up straighter in his seat.

"There are many places that need my attention at the moment," Natta replied, sitting down next to her father.

"You made good time," Kubo murmured.

Natta glanced at Ash before she replied. "I wanted to see for myself if it was true," she replied in a quiet tone.

"If what was true?" Ash asked.

Natta hesitated; her gaze was focused on a woman walking toward them with a drink in each hand. His gaze followed Natta's and softened. It would appear that Kella came bearing a drink as a way of saying she was sorry for kicking his ass – though he'd never admit that she had.

"Drink. It will help hide your pain," Kella said, holding out the green liquor and sitting down next to him.

"Hide it or make it better?" Ash teased, taking the glass and looking suspiciously at the liquid in it. "What is it?"

"*Tusku pissata,*" Kella replied.

Ash sniffed it and shrugged. It smelled like alcohol. He took a sip. A hoarse cough escaped him when it burned a path down his throat. He lifted a hand to wipe at the moisture that formed in his eyes and shook his head.

Hell, if I finish this, I won't be feeling anything, he thought.

He watched in disbelief as Kella tipped her glass and swallowed half the liquid in a single gulp. She wiped a hand across her mouth and sat back with a satisfied smile on her face. Ash glanced down at his glass and lowered it. The fire that had been in his throat was now burning in his stomach.

"What is *Tusku pissata*?" he asked in a hoarse voice. "I mean, I know it is your form of liquor, but this stuff is more like one hundred proof moonshine."

"Tusku are very large beasts on Tesla Terra. They are very mean," Natta laughed.

"Pissata is piss. A trader many years ago discovered if you fermented their urine and mixed it with some of the grains from the plants here, it makes strong liquor. It is a favorite among the travelers here at the Spaceport and only made here," Kella explained.

"You mean, I just drank some animal's urine?" Ash asked in disgust.

"How do you know about the *Tusku Pissata*?" Natta asked.

Ash turned in surprised at the bite to Natta's voice. She was staring at Kella. He glanced at Kella.

She appeared relaxed, but he saw her left hand drop down to her side and she fingered the handle of one of the blades she wore. He dropped his hand down and covered hers. She stiffened for a moment before she relaxed.

"It is a popular drink," Kella replied.

"Natta has discovered where Hutu and those with them have gone," Kubo announced with a proud grin.

Natta snorted in disapproval at her father's enjoyment. "There will be repercussions from Hutu's act, Father."

Ash started to set his drink down, but Kella drained her glass and reached for his. He handed it to her with a skeptical shake of his head before returning his attention to Natta. She glanced suspiciously at Kella before she reluctantly continued.

"Word is spreading that Hutu and two others boarded General Landais' Battle Cruiser," Natta said.

"Whoa, is that the really bad-ass guy for the Legion?" Ash asked in disbelief.

Kubo chuckled while Natta just nodded. "Packu de Rola was captured. He is the eldest son of Jemar de Rola, a former Knight of the Gallant Order and close friend of Hutu. Jemar and his youngest son, Jesup, were murdered by the Legion and their vineyard was burned to the ground. Rumor has it that the Legion commander found a capsule and is searching for its contents. Those contents, in the form of a stranger from another world, defeated the Legion forces and killed the commander before he and Cassa de Rola escaped over the mountains to where my son lived," Kubo explained.

"The capsule... It must have been Josh's.... But... How did they end up here?" Ash asked, searching Kubo and Natta's faces.

"The signal from your capsule was tracked to the desert. Hutu recognized the significance of it. He would also need to hide Cassa and the stranger – Josh – from the Legion. He came here to find you. We are also the eyes and ears of the galaxy. Jeslean is the original home of the Gallant Order, but the Legion has all but isolated it from the rest of the star systems. A new, temporary headquarters was established on one of the moons orbiting Tesla Terra," Kubo continued.

"Father...," Natta murmured, glancing again at Kella. "Perhaps we should not be discussing this here."

Kella drained the second glass and placed it on the table with a loud thump. She pulled her hand away from Ash and stood up. He started to rise, but she held her hand out for him to stay where he was.

"I have things to do. I will be in the quarters you assigned me," Kella said.

"Kella...," Ash murmured, reaching out a hand to her.

She turned to look at him with a cool expression that faded when she saw he was genuinely concerned. Once again, he saw a flash of emotion in her eyes, as if she wasn't sure what to do. She shook her head.

"I will speak with you later," she promised before turning and walking away.

Ash watched her go, a slow anger burning inside him. He had seen the looks of suspicion and distrust cast at Kella over the last two days. Whatever issue people had with Kella, they would have to get over it. Ash drew in a deep, calming breath and redirected his attention to Kubo and Natta. There were certain battles he needed to pick, and this was not one of them – yet.

"What the hell is going on?" Ash demanded.

Kubo sat back in his seat. "Hutu, Cassa, and Josh stole a Legion supply ship, boarded General Landais' personal Battle Cruiser, and freed Packu de Rola from the prison cells aboard it before disabling the Battle Cruiser and escaping."

Ash blinked, absorbing what Kubo just said. He knew that move. It was a classic military strategy studied by students in middle school. Hell, he and Josh used the same principle once during a mission.

"The Trojan Horse," he chuckled with a shake of his head. "He used the damn Trojan Horse to get on board."

"You recognize how they were able to accomplish such a thing?" Natta asked in surprise.

Ash nodded. "Hell, yeah. Josh and I did the same damn thing on one of our missions back home. We caught holy hell for it, but we got the men out from behind enemy lines, so we got a medal for it too," he replied.

A sense of relief and excitement built inside him. For the first time, the realization washed through him that at least one other member of the Gliese had made it. Yes, he had known that the description of the man sounded like Josh, but there was still that feeling of disbelief. This daring act, though, was a classic maneuver from their past.

"I need a way to this moon you were talking about," Ash said.

Kubo released a sigh. "I agree, but it will be dangerous. Come, walk with me, Ashton Haze," Kubo said, rising from his seat.

"Father…," Natta began, standing as well.

"All will be fine, Natta," Kubo reassured his daughter.

Natta bowed her head. "If you say so," she murmured. "I will say good rest to you both."

"Goodnight, Natta," Ash said, standing and waiting for Kubo.

Ash silently followed Kubo out of the dining area and through a maze of tunnels. The elaborate passages wound for miles and miles under the surface of the planet. Most of the tunnels were carved by the underground rivers, while others were expanded by centuries of Torrians living in the naturally created caverns.

The rooms where he was staying were in the dwellings of Kubo and his extended family. Ash ran his gaze over the paintings and sculptures decorating the walls and rooms. Most of them appeared to depict the history of the Torrians. He paused when he saw one that showed a dozen men, each standing with long staffs in their hands and wearing elegant robes.

"What do you see?" Kubo asked, stopping in the corridor when he sensed Ash's hesitation.

Ash studied the illustration. "Honestly? It's like something out of a movie or from the time of King Arthur and the Knights of the Round Table," he replied.

Kubo released a sigh. "I am the third one from the right," he said in a quiet voice.

"You! You were a Knight of the Gallant Order?" Ash asked in surprise, turning to look at Kubo.

"I was not always old, Ashton Haze, or blind. How do you think Hutu learned to be a knight? There were twelve of us, then; far fewer than there were before our time. We were the guardians of the Gallant Order. Our mission was to oversee the peace among the different worlds under our protection. We trained our sons and daughters to follow in our footsteps. Hutu is my eldest child and became a Knight of the Gallant order at a very young age. I am training Natta. She is still young, but grows more skilled each day," Kubo murmured, staring at the wall as if he could see the images painted on the stone.

"What happened?" Ash asked.

"Peace… and a belief that the Knights of the Gallant Order were no longer needed to serve the council. The culture of the Knights was abandoned by most of the new ruling class. This movement was led by a young counselor. Soon, the Knights began to die in mysterious accidents. Those who resisted found they were not the only targets, but their families were as well," Kubo murmured.

Ash could hear the sound of grief mixed in Kubo's voice. He turned to gaze at the painting. There was something powerful in it, noble and majestic.

"They came after your family?" Ash quietly asked.

Kubo nodded. "Hutu was not my only son," he replied, turning away from the painting. "Come."

Ash followed Kubo down the passage to the end where a large set of carved doors blocked them from going farther. Kubo held out his walking stick to Ash. Ash gripped the stick and watched Kubo unlock the door using an old key. He held out the walking stick to Kubo and stepped back when the other man pulled the door open.

Behind the doors was a large cavern with a vaulted ceiling. Dim lights came on, lighting the area as they walked forward. Ash quickly realized that this was a catacomb. He shivered when an icy draft swirled around him. The temperature in the room was cold enough that he could see his breath when he exhaled.

"What are we doing here?" he asked.

Kubo continued walking down the aisle between the sarcophagi. Ash ran his gaze over the walls as they threaded their way deeper into the room. He could see small lights glowing from those buried in crypts along the walls of the cavern. He returned his attention to a large sarcophagus placed at an angle in the center of the room. It took a moment for Ash to realize that all the center sarcophagi were placed in a circular formation.

He swallowed when Kubo laid a trembling hand on the carved top. Kubo released a sigh before dropping his hand and moving to the next tomb. Ash glanced at the face of the figure on the first one and realized it was of a woman.

"My mate," Kubo said before Ash could ask. "And our son."

Ash stepped closer to look at the mask that was created in the likeness of Kubo's son. He looked a lot like the old man, but younger. The figure was wearing a cloak similar to those in the painting. His hands were folded, but in between them was a metal pole which Ash recognized immediately as one of the staffs the Knights carried.

Kubo's hand ran along the tomb, gently tracing the features of the carved image before continuing down its side. When he reached the staff, he pulled it free. Ash watched Kubo turn the elegantly detailed cylinder of metal in his hands before he held it out to Ash.

"This belongs to you, Ashton Haze," Kubo said.

Ash took a step back. "Kubo… I can't…," he started to protest.

Kubo's finger slid over it and he reached for Ash's hand. Ash felt Kubo's cold fingers wrap around his right wrist. His gaze followed Kubo as the old man placed the cylinder in the palm of his hand. His fingers closed around the metal. Ash jerked when he felt a slight shock from the staff.

"It is now yours, Ashton Haze. You must accept your place in this world – and your position as a Knight of the Gallant Order," Kubo said.

"Kubo… This isn't my fight," Ash protested, shaking his head back and forth even as he gripped the Staff in his hand.

Kubo's eyes glistened and his voice trembled. This was uncharacteristic of the old man who almost always had a mischievous expression on his face. Ash could feel his head shaking back and forth even as he gripped the staff in his hand.

"Would you leave our world without hope? The Legion has attacked Jeslean. It is a peaceful world, home of the Ancient Gallant Order, and of the Gallant ruling council. Director Andronikos ordered the destruction of the major cities, including the capital. Hundreds of thousands of innocent men, women, and children of all species were brutally killed without warning. Andronikos has made a statement to all the star systems; he will wipe out any who try to resist him, and hurt the innocent in order to strike fear in the hearts of those who stand against him." Kubo drew in a breath, and when he spoke again, his voice was infused with a quiet strength. "You and your friends bring hope. You have awakened a force that will not be extinguished."

Ash swallowed. He looked around the dim interior before his gaze settled on the tomb of Kubo's son and Knight of the Gallant Order. Ash said this wasn't his war, but his and Josh's presence had already ignited a firestorm. Josh's involvement in a mission demonstrated that he wasn't backing down and hiding. It had never been their way.

"I never did like dictators or bullies," Ash said.

"I did not think you would. Now, I will show you how a Knight of the Gallant fights," Kubo replied.

Kubo walked by him, the old man's hand reaching out to run along the tomb of his mate. With a silent expletive, Ash followed Kubo out of the cavern.

Chapter 15

Several hours later, Ash walked the corridors. His mind was buzzing from everything he learned. Sleep was the last thing he felt like doing at the moment.

Kubo had shown him how the Staff worked. The shock he felt was a way of imprinting the device to his specific genetic markers. Kubo explained that each Staff was programmed for a specific user. It could be passed down, but in order to do so safely, the original owner or another Knight must pass the Staff on to the new member. This ensured the technology behind it remained a secret.

Ash spent several hours learning how the Staff worked. It shocked and amazed him – two things he should be over by now. Hell, those two feelings had been with him since he first woke up in the desert.

Lifting a hand, he ran it over his damp hair. He had gone back to his room, showered, and tried to sleep, but it had been impossible. After an hour of tossing and turning, he gave up, dressed, and decided a long walk might help. It took a few minutes to realize that his feet were taking him in the direction of Kella's quarters.

He slowed when he neared the door to her room. He was surprised to find it partially open. He raised his hand to knock, but froze when he saw her doing one of the katas he showed her earlier. She was wearing a short, tan top with low hanging wide-bottom pants similar to those he saw some of the women here wearing.

Swallowing, he quietly stood watching her. There was one part she was having trouble with and kept repeating. His lips twitched when she released a growl of frustration and stomped her feet before moving back into position to try again.

Unable to just observe, he quietly stepped into the room and moved up behind her. Copying her stance, he extended his arm, allowing her to see him before he slid his hand along her arm and moved it back ever so slightly so that her elbow was closer to her side. He pressed his body against hers so he could lead her.

Together, they moved as one. When Kella reached the part that she was having difficulty with, Ash took over, guiding her through the moves. Her breath caught and he could sense her excitement. He stepped back and to the side when she finished the kata.

Kella smiled and moved into position. They both bowed before they began doing the kata over again. Almost half an hour passed before Kella laughed and twirled to face him. Her face glowed with delight.

"I have never felt so much power within my body and mind before. It was as if… as if I was one with the energy around me," Kella said excitedly before the smile on her lips faded.

Ash stepped closer and lifted his hand to run his fingers down her cheek. His gaze swept over her face and he had an uncontrollable urge to kiss her. He slid his hand down to her chin and tilted her head back so that he could look into her eyes.

"You are beautiful when you laugh," he murmured, brushing his thumb along her lower lip.

"It is the first time I ever remember doing that," she admitted in a soft voice.

Ash frowned in confusion. "Doing what?"

"Laughing," she replied.

Ash stared at Kella in disbelief. The words told him a lot about what her life must have been like growing up. His life had been filled with laughter. Sure, there had been some bad days, but his grandmother had a wicked sense of humor and believed that laughter was a positive healer for both your physical body and your mental soul. He couldn't imagine a life of never seeing the bright side of things.

"Well, I think you have a lot of catching up to do," he teased before his eyes grew dark with desire. "I really want to kiss you, Kella."

She raised an eyebrow and her lips curved in amusement. "You do? How much is the 'really want to' worth to you?" she quipped.

It took a second for Ash to realize she was teasing him. He chuckled softly and stepped closer to her, sliding his hand along her cheek to the back of her neck. He paused a breath away from her lips.

"How about you tell me?" he retorted in a low voice before he captured her lips.

"I would rather show you," she murmured with a mischievous smile.

Ash released a hissing breath when her hand slid down the front of his body. Damn, but he loved a woman who knew what she wanted and wasn't afraid to take it – in this case him. Reaching down, he grabbed the hem of her shirt and pulled it off. Tonight was going to be a long, long night – in the most pleasurable ways if he had his way.

* * *

Kella blinked the next morning. Her hand stretched out along her bed. Ash was gone. Sitting up, she pulled the covers around her and glanced around. A smile curved her lips when she saw the tray with fresh fruit, bread, cheeses, and a covered drink on the small table.

Sliding out of bed, she walked across to the 'bathroom' as Ash called it. Taking a quick shower and dressing, Kella sat down at the table and pulled the cover off the drink before lifting it to her lips to take a sip. Her gaze moved over the table. There were two plates. Something told her Ash would be back.

She thought of their night together. He had made her feel beautiful. The things he did to her left her breathless one moment and on fire the next. Her lips curved up when she remembered doing the same to him.

She might not have had the experience, but she wasn't shy about learning new things. He taught her how to pleasure him and in return, she found joy in discovering her own desires. The biggest thing Kella learned last night was that her mentor was wrong. There are some things, some people in this world, who should be treasured, and Ash was one of them.

"You're awake!" Ash said, pushing the door open with his foot before kicking it closed behind him.

Kella rose from her chair and looked at him with a bemused expression when she saw the amount of food on the second tray he was carrying. He walked across the room, an intense look of concentration on his face as he tried not to spill anything. It took a moment to realize there was a brilliant flower in the center of the tray.

"Are you planning on eating the flower as well?" she asked, reaching over and picking it up.

Ash scowled at her. "No, it is for you," he said with a grin. "I know you get hungry. I was planning on serving you breakfast in bed, but now that you are up, we can eat at the table."

"Breakfast in bed?" she asked, glancing at the unmade bed and then the tray.

"It sounds great, but it is hard as hell to eat without making a mess and there is nothing worse than trying to sleep in a pile of crumbs," he said.

It was Kella's turn to scowl. "You have done this for other women?" she asked, lifting the flower to her nose and sniffing it.

Ash nodded. "I tried to do it whenever I was home for my grandmother. It was a running joke between us. I was about seven when I brought it to her one Saturday morning. I burned the toast, undercooked the eggs, and had a bowl of cereal filled to the top. We sat in the middle of her bed and ate it all," he replied, placing the tray on the table. "I'm a better cook now."

Kella chuckled when she saw the prepared food. "You did not make that," she said, sliding back into her chair.

"Nope, but I carried it all the way from the kitchens," Ash declared.

Kella looked at the bounty of food. Her stomach growled in appreciation of his efforts. It all looked fabulous. She felt the strange burning in her eyes and nose. Her gaze moved to the flower in her hand – and the burning intensified.

"Why did you do this?" she asked, looking up at him.

The easy grin on his face faded to be replaced by an intense expression. He studied her face for several long seconds before he reached his right hand across the table. Kella frowned at the gesture before she placed her hand in his.

"Because you deserve it and I wanted to. Last night was incredible, Kella. I hope you felt it too. I... I'm very attracted to you," he admitted.

Kella tilted her head and studied him in return. Last night was more than incredible – if there was such a thing. Unable to express the feelings raging inside her, Kella squeezed his hand and pulled back, lifting the flower to her nose again.

"I want to have more nights like last night," she murmured, not looking at him.

His low chuckle told her that he heard her statement. "Well, if you want more nights like last night, I'd better feed you," he replied.

Her stomach chose that moment to growl loudly. They both laughed. Kella placed the flower down next to her plate and began to fill it with all the delicious looking food.

"I would like to learn more about your self-defense moves. There are many that are similar to what I have learned, but others that are different. The way you execute them is also very different," she said around a mouthful of food.

"You were doing a few things I wouldn't mind learning either," Ash replied. "I'd like to find out if Kubo has discovered any new information."

"I will need to check on my freighter," Kella said. "I paid a young boy to watch over it. I do not imagine he is still there."

The spork in Ash's hand froze halfway to his mouth. "It is too dangerous for you to go above ground," he warned. "I'll ask Kubo if he can send someone to check on it."

Kella opened her mouth to protest, but the glimmer of warning in his eyes and the realization that he was correct in his assessment of the danger silenced her. She was not used to this type of behavior. It shouldn't matter that it was dangerous. She would move in the shadows of the city anyway. Her ability to change her appearance was definitely a strategy in her favor.

"By the way, how did you do that yesterday?" Ash asked, leaning forward.

Kella blinked in surprise. "How did I do what?" she asked.

Ash waved his hand in a circle while pointing it at her. "You know, change your skin color. One minute you were dark green, the next you looked like all the other Torrians with the red skin and tattoo lines," he replied.

"It is one of the reasons Tallei chose me as her pupil. I can change my appearance. It makes me a… It allows me to blend in so I can move among other species easier. If anyone looks hard enough, they will see I am different, but most only look at the obvious," Kella explained with a shrugged.

Ash grinned. "That is really amazing," he said.

Kella smiled and lowered her gaze. She did not lie to him – she was just not completely honest. It was one of the reasons that Tallei chose her and it did help her blend in. She used it as a way to get closer to her targets or to avoid capture. For now, she would listen, learn, and enjoy her time with Ash – for as long as she could before he discovered who and what she really was.

Chapter 16

Two days later, the feel of Kella's body stiffening and the sound of the door scraping on the floor alerted Ash to the fact they were no longer alone. His fingers closed over Kella's when her hand moved to the blade she had hidden between the wall and the mattress. Lifting his head, he peered over her shoulder.

"Father says you both must come to the great hall," Natta stated from the doorway.

Ash threaded his fingers through Kella's and nodded. "Tell him we'll be there in ten minutes," he said.

Natta tilted her head and stared at the two of them for a moment before she shook her head and turned on her heel. She glanced over her shoulder once more before she closed the door behind her. Only when she was gone did he feel Kella's body relax.

"Note to self, make sure I announce myself before I enter a room with you in it," Ash chuckled, releasing her hand and leaning up so he could gaze down at her. "Good morning, beautiful."

Kella's eyes twinkled with mischief. Ash should have known she was up to something when her other hand curled over his right buttock and she squeezed it. A low curse escaped him when his body immediately responded.

"You will greet me each morning with that phrase, in addition to the breakfast on a tray. I like it," she said.

"Darling, if we had more than ten minutes, I'd be greeting you another way," Ash swore, dropping a quick kiss to her lips.

"I would like that very much as well. You are very different from the men who came to Tallei's bar, Ash. I am very grateful for that," Kella replied, lifting her free hand to touch his face.

"I'll take that as a compliment. We'd better get moving or we'll both end up standing in front of that old man in our birthday suits. I don't care what anyone says, I still don't believe he is as blind as he acts," Ash dryly commented before he kissed the tip of her nose, pulled away, and slid off the other side of the bed.

"I was wondering if he was," Kella remarked, throwing the covers back and sliding out of the bed as well.

Ash turned in time to see Kella walk across the room to pick up the clothing that was cleaned for her. He bit back a groan of frustration. His body was on full alert now that he broke his celibacy. Why couldn't they both be marooned on a tropical desert island with five star service – the kind with the little colorful umbrellas and a queen size hammock between two palm trees?

"Ash... Ash.... Are you well?" Kella asked with a raised eyebrow.

Ash blinked. It took him a minute to realize he was just standing there, naked as the day he was born, with a goofy grin on his face. He nodded and walked over to pick his clothes up from the floor that he discarded the night before. He stepped into his trousers, pulled them up, and fastened them so they would not fall off before tugging his shirt over his head. He really should just move the few items he had from his room into Kella's since that is where he'd spent his last two nights.

"I need to stop by my room for some real clothes," he said.

"I will meet you in the great room," Kella replied.

"Sounds good," Ash said, walking by her and dropping a quick, hard kiss to her lips. "Good morning, beautiful."

He ran his hand over the curve of her buttock before he continued out the door. A happy grin curved his lips when he heard her muttered curse behind him. The icy reserve was definitely melted and he planned to keep it that way.

Whistling a popular tune from back home, he broke into a jog. His body and mind were humming. This new life may not be so bad after all, he thought as he ran back to his quarters to change.

..*

Kella stepped out of her room and began walking down the passage to meet with Ash and Kubo. Her footsteps slowed when she saw the Torrian female who entered her room a short while ago standing at the end of the corridor watching her. Lifting her head, she looked back at the woman with an unwavering stare.

Natta straightened when Kella drew even with her. Kella didn't slow down. She also didn't miss the flash of irritation on the other woman's face.

"I wanted to talk to you," Natta stated.

Kella shrugged. "So does your father. He is your leader; I will listen to what he has to say," she replied, ignoring the other woman when she stopped.

"Do you really think you are good enough for a Knight of the Gallant Order?" Natta suddenly asked.

Kella slowed to a stop and turned to face the other woman. Her fingers moved to the grip of her laser pistol. She didn't miss the other woman's wary step back or the fact that she fingered her own weapon by her side. Kella saw the intricately carved cylinder. Her lips tightened.

"That is not your concern, Torrian. It matters not whether you think I am good enough or not," Kella replied, staring the other woman down.

"He will just use you and toss you aside when he knows what you are," Natta retorted.

Kella relaxed her shoulders and allowed a mocking smile to curve her lips. "What makes you think he doesn't already know?" she asked.

A flicker of doubt crossed Natta's face. Satisfied that she had won this small battle, Kella turned on her heel and strode away. Natta didn't see the doubt or apprehension swirling through Kella, nor did the woman see the knife Kella had drawn in case she needed it.

Kella refused to allow Natta or anyone else to see the pain the other woman's words caused her. Was this what Tallei meant when she said caring for something would make her weak? Deep down, Kella knew that Ash didn't really know who, or what, she was. It was obvious from his words. She knew that if she didn't tell him, someone else would, but she couldn't bear it if he looked at her with the same distrust, fear, and disgust that many of the others did.

The Turbinta were good enough to kill for other species, but they were considered expendable after they were no longer needed. Tallei told her as much. Their code was to live for the kill, collect the credits and stay alive long enough to become a mentor.

Suddenly, none of that sounded good – or right – any longer. It seemed as if everything that Kella had ever known was a lie. The world was not a bad place; well, not all of it. There were good people in it. People like Abeni and Noma and Kubo and… Ash. There were things that were funny and things that were beautiful.

And things that were incredible, Kella thought, thinking of the night before as she entered the large dining hall.

Kubo sat over to the side on one of the plush couches. He held his long walking stick in his hands. For the first time, Kella studied the old man's face. She realized that the lines on it told a story.

Walking closer, she analyzed his face and learned bits and pieces about his life. There were wrinkles by the corner of his eyes and his mouth that told her he had laughed and smiled a lot. Yet, he also had lines across his brow and under his eyes as if he had felt great sorrow or worry.

"You study me as if you are unsure of your welcome, Kella of the Turbinta," Kubo said in a gentle tone.

"How did you know it was me?" Kella asked curiously.

"You walk very quietly, much differently than many of the others here who stomp their feet to make sure I do not step on them," Kubo chuckled in response.

Kubo patted the seat next to him and waited for her to sit down. Kella glanced around the open dining area. There were only a handful of people in the room. She noticed that one or more would look in their direction before glancing away.

"They care about you. They are afraid I will harm you," she murmured.

"Yes," Kubo acknowledged.

Kella stiffened and sat up straighter. "I won't," she said.

Kubo reached over and patted her hand. "I know you won't, child. Regardless of what you may have been taught, your heart is still pure," he murmured.

Kella looked down at the hand covering hers. An unfamiliar burning made her eyes ache. She blinked to clear it, but the burning continued. Curling her fingers into a fist, she willed the strange feeling to go away.

"How can you be sure? Tallei said...," Kella's voice faded when she saw Ash entering the room.

Kubo patted Kella's hand again. "Your mentor picked the wrong pupil when she stole you away, Kella. Your people are kind and gentle, but they are also fiercely protective of their own. Tallei hoped to train that out of you, but she failed," he said.

"You know who my people are?" Kella whispered, staring at Kubo in shock.

"Yes."

Kella blinked, forcing her gaze away from Kubo's serene face. She glanced at Ash. Natta was walking beside him. His face looked taut and there was a hint of anger on it. Kella quickly glanced down. If Natta told Ash about her – about what a Turbinta really was – she would slit the woman's throat in her sleep.

Her hands trembled. She wasn't ready to deal with Ash looking at her the way the others did, not yet; especially after what happened between them last night. The burning was back in her eyes, this time stronger than before.

She drew in a deep breath when she felt the cushion next to her sink down. It wasn't until a strong, dark hand curled around hers that she looked up in surprise. Ash winked at her and pulled her hand up to his lips to press a kiss to the back of it.

"Sorry, it took me a little longer than I expected," he said.

Kella nodded and shot a quick glance over at Natta's stony expression. A pleased feeling flooded her. She looked up at Ash. His gaze was the warm, reassuring one he gave her earlier. Either Natta didn't tell him about what it meant to be a Turbinta or Ash didn't cared.

"I have received disturbing news," Kubo stated.

"What is it?" Ash asked, leaning forward so he could see Kubo's face.

"The Legion is planning to attack Tesla Terra. This time, they plan to destroy all the cities on the planet. It will be the ultimate example of what is to come, I'm afraid," Kubo replied with a deep sigh.

Kella frowned. "Can you not warn them? They can start evacuation procedures, move from the city, something," she said.

"We can't," Natta said. "The Legion forces are jamming our signals. They have placed a ban on all outgoing flights. Any ship caught trying to leave the planet will either be stopped or destroyed."

"There has to be some way to warn them," Ash said.

"I fear the rebellion may be over before it has even begun," Kubo remarked in a suddenly tired voice.

"Father," Natta murmured in concern, rising to her feet and coming to stand near him.

"If there was a way to go myself, I would," Kubo murmured.

"I could go," Kella hesitantly suggested.

Natta turned to gaze at Kella in shock. "How? The Legion has the entire planet locked down," she demanded.

"I would leave the same way I came in. My freighter is stored on the outskirts of the city. I would cut through the mountain passes, keeping low until I reach the Sand Deserts on the far side. The Legion does not have the resources to stop all transports," Kella stated.

Natta shook her head. "The only people crazy enough to try that route are the pirates. The area is littered with spaceships that have tried and failed. There are only a few handfuls of ships that have ever made it through the canyons unscathed," she retorted.

Kella nodded. "Yes… and I am one of them," she replied in a calm, confident voice.

Kubo picked up Kella's left hand and held it tightly in his. She could feel the slight tremble in it. Her fingers curled around his and she gently squeezed them to show him she understood.

"Tell us what you need," Kubo instructed.

Chapter 17

Several hours later, Natta, Kella, Ash, and three of Kubo's elite guards peered down from a rock outcropping. Ash decided the entire planet had to be riddled with underground passages and hidden entrances. They just popped out from one that led them to the outer rim of the landing site where Kella's freighter was docked.

"Which one is yours?" Natta asked, scanning the area.

"Fourth row, third one from the end," Kella murmured.

Ash lowered the rifle he was carrying and propped it on the rock next to him. Next, he shrugged his backpack off his shoulder. He reached for the binoculars in the side pouch. Lifting them to his eyes, he aimed them on the spaceport below and adjusted the focus.

His gaze swept down the rows to the fourth one and then moved over to the end until he reached Kella's spaceship. He must have reached her ship at the same time as the others from the chorus of grunts and snorts that burst out next to him. Natta pulled her viewing glasses down and turned to look at Kella with a raised eyebrow and a very doubtful expression.

"Please tell me you are not serious. I do not know how to fly a spaceship yet, but even I know that ship is nothing more than a death trap," Natta stated.

Kella shot Natta a heated glare. "It is fast," she said.

"It is small," Natta retorted.

"It has to be to get through the canyons," Kella replied.

"It looks like it will fall apart before it escapes our atmosphere. This will not work. We must think of another plan," Natta snapped and turned away.

Ash laid his hand on Kella's arm when she started to protest. She turned to look at him and he could see the resentment and hurt in Kella's eyes. He knew the feeling. Sometimes you just connected with the plane – or in this case, spaceship.

"Will it hold together?" Ash asked in a quiet voice.

Kella nodded. "I know every bolt on that ship. It will get us out of here," she promised.

"If you say it will, then it will. Let's go," Ash said.

Kella's eyes widened with surprise before narrowing with determination. She gave him a brief nod and stood up. Together, they turned and began threading their way down the rocks.

..*

"Father will think of another plan," Natta said while she motioned the guards with them to return through the entrance.

She turned to motion for Ash and Kella to go next only to find they were no longer there. Turning, she released an exasperated snort. One of the guards turned back in concern and frowned when he saw what happened.

"Do you wish for me to go with them?" he asked.

Natta shook her head and a reluctant smile curved her lips. "No, something tells me they will be fine. We have work to do here," she said, watching the two figures blend in with the other workers down below.

..*

Ash motioned for Kella to slow down. They both turned and began acting like they were talking to each other when a Legion soldier walked by. From what they had seen so far, there weren't very many in this area. They either already did an inspection or were spread too thin to care about what looked more like a spaceship junkyard than a spaceport.

"This way," Kella murmured, turning and walking along the dilapidated vessels.

They walked side by side. Ash couldn't help but feel a wave of indecision. He glanced at Kella, but she didn't appear to be having the same doubts. He honestly hoped her freighter looked better up close than it did from a distance.

His hopes were dashed when Kella turned left and walked over to a dark gray spaceship with long streaks of black along the sides. He followed her, glancing over his shoulder to make sure they didn't attract any attention. Kella opened a panel near the back and pressed in a code before closing the panel. A platform next to the panel began to lower. It made it halfway down before it stopped.

"Argh! I thought I fixed that," Kella cursed under her breath.

"Thought... What do you mean you fixed it? Don't you have mechanics and engineers to do the repairs? You know... someone who is certified in spaceships?" Ash asked, following her around to the side of the ship.

"I am the mechanic. It is my ship. No one touches it but me," she growled.

"I understand, but.... What are you doing?" Ash asked.

Kella walked over to a pile of discarded parts. She rummaged through the pile, picking up assorted pieces. She examined each piece before she tossed them aside. She continued searching the junk pile until she found two long pieces of metal pipe. He watched as she weighed each piece of pipe in her hands before she threw the one in her right hand back onto the pile and turned around.

Once again, Ash followed her. His eyes widened and his hand lifted in protest when he saw her grip one end like a bat and swing it at the hydraulic joint. Her whole body shook from the reverberation when metal struck metal. She struck the joint two more times before he was able to rip the pipe out of her hands.

"What... are... you... doing?" Ash asked in a slow, measured, exasperated tone.

"Repairing it," Kella said, placing her hands on her hips.

"Repairing.... Are you crazy? Beating the shit out of a complicated piece of equipment that goes into space is not repairing it!" he retorted.

The words no sooner left his mouth than the platform kicked into gear and lowered to the ground. He shook his head when Kella gave him a triumphant look. She looked so damn cute, he wanted to kiss her.

"You there! What are you doing?" a voice called out behind them.

Ash didn't think. He threw the pipe he was holding with deadly accuracy. Ash winced when the man's head snapped backwards. He watched in slow motion as the soldier's eyes rolled back in his head and he collapsed.

"Well, shit," Ash swore.

Kella stared down at the soldier for a moment before she turned to look at him. A huge grin curved her lips and her eyes glowed with admiration. He shook his head when he heard what sounded suspiciously like a chuckle escape her.

"That was very good," she said.

"Has anyone ever told you that you are a blood-thirsty woman?" he asked.

Kella nodded. "Yes... you," she retorted with another laugh.

"Help me hide him. We need to get out of here before anyone sees what's happened," he grunted.

He walked by her and bent to grab the man's arms. Kella picked up the soldier's feet. They carried the body over and hid it behind the pile of discarded junk that Kella was searching through just minutes before. Ash came to the conclusion that life would never be boring again as he wiped his hands together.

"I will start the engines while you release the locks," Kella instructed.

Ash reached out and touched her arm. He waited until she looked at him. Doubt and concern clouded his expression.

"Are you sure this thing can get us out of here?" he asked in a somber tone.

Her expression softened and she reached forward to brush a kiss across his lips. "Yes," she replied.

Ash watched her turn and scoop up the soldier's fallen laser rifle before she hurried up the ramp. Releasing a long sigh, he turned and focused on releasing the locks. He really hoped that the engines were in better shape than the rest of the ship. Hell, he hoped the hull was in better shape than it looked or it wouldn't matter about the Legion, the engines, the canyon, or the ramp! If the hull breached, they would be popping louder than a can of biscuits on a warm Sunday morning and oozing out of the seams.

"That is not the picture I need in my head at the moment," Ash muttered.

He released the last lock and strode around the ship to the platform. He groaned when he saw two more soldiers walking toward the ship. The damn Legion was like a mosquito, every time you thought you killed the last one, another one – or in this case two – appeared.

"Damn it all to hell," he cursed, swinging around and jogging up the platform. "Kella! We've got company coming," he shouted.

He turned, eyeing the men who had picked up their pace. Ash searched for the control to close the platform. He could feel the rumble of the engines powering up under his feet. His gaze focused on a red button next to the opening. He slammed his palm on it at the same time as one of the soldiers lifted the rifle to his shoulder.

"Close, damn it!" Ash snarled.

He shrugged off the rifle on his shoulder and fired from the hip. Not the best plan of action, but the only choice he had. The first shot hit the soldier on the right in the chest while the second blast spun the other soldier around. He didn't have time to fire again before the platform blocked his view.

He stumbled to the side and reached for a support beam to steady himself when the freighter began to rise off the ground. A loud curse exploded from his lips when the platform stopped halfway again. Turning, he placed the rifle up against the side under the control for the ramp. Right next to where he set the gun was a long metal bar. With a shake of his head, he held onto the beam and reached for the pipe.

Raising the pipe, he swung as hard as he could at the hydraulic power. The force of the blow reverberated down his arm. He couldn't tell over the sound of the engines if it was going to work. Drawing back his arm, he was about to hit the joint again when the platform suddenly began moving.

"Ash, we have company coming. I need you to get buckled in," Kella's voice echoed over the intercom system.

He turned and replaced the pipe, grabbed the rifle, shrugged off his backpack, and took off across the storage area to a doorway across from it. He stumbled and bounced off the framing around the door when the freighter tilted to the side. A long list of colorful words that he hadn't said since he was a kid escaped him, followed almost immediately by the disapproving image of his grandmother's face.

"Sorry, Grandma," he muttered, holding onto the wall and trying to stay on his feet. "Kella! Where in the hell do I go?"

"This way!" Kella yelled back.

Ash followed the sound of her voice. It would appear that the corridor was a straight shot to the front of the freighter. Up ahead, he saw a short set of stairs. He sprinted forward.

He grabbed the railing and his body swiveled almost one hundred and eighty degrees when the freighter suddenly turned at an angle. Such a maneuver would have been impossible for anything back home except maybe a helicopter. He sat down and braced his feet when the freighter suddenly shot forward, throwing him back against the steps. Pain lanced through the center of his back where the edge of the metal step bit into his flesh. His head snapped back and he gritted his teeth.

"Bloody hell!" he snapped.

His arms strained to hold on until the ship leveled off enough for him to twist around and stand. He really wished he had more time to savor seeing the cockpit of an alien spaceship. Unfortunately, his eyes were not on the controls, or even Kella, but on the rapidly approaching hole in the mountains.

"You need to buckle up, this is going to be tight," Kella instructed loudly, glancing over her shoulder.

"Tight?! You call that tight? You need a bigger hole if you plan on taking this thing through it," Ash retorted in a tight voice.

He staggered and half fell into the co-pilot seat. His eyes remained glued to the dark hole they were approaching even as his hands frantically fumbled with the unfamiliar straps of the seat harness. The sound of the buckle clicking registered in his mind and his hands dropped to the armrest.

Kella shot him a brief look. An amused smile curved her lips. Ash ignored her. He was afraid to take his eyes off the ever-narrowing distance between them and certain death.

An explosion of rocks rained down from near the entrance. Ash pressed back against his seat as the freighter swept through the entrance. Above him, Ash could see the fragments of basketball size rocks raining against the thick clear view screen of the ship. The sound was abnormally loud, perhaps due to his fear and the enclosed space. Darkness swallowed them, blinding them for a moment before a glow of red lights lit the area in front of them.

"The tunnel, Kella. The tunnel is ending… Kella, I hate to tell you this, but the tunnel is ending…," Ash urgently chanted, seeing nothing but a wall of rock in front of them.

"No, it isn't," she replied, pressing the controls forward.

The freighter tilted and the nose turned down. It took Ash a moment to realize that it was an optical illusion. The tunnel actually curved downward. The freighter dipped, skimming the floor of the tunnel before shooting forward out the other end and into a long, equally narrow canyon. Ash glanced up at the screen in front of them. The two blips that were following them on the screen suddenly disappeared.

"Where in the hell did you learn about that?" Ash asked in a hoarse voice.

"There were a lot of freighter pilots who came to Tallei's bar over the years. Tallei told me the reason she opened a bar was to gather information. It helps when…." Kella paused before continuing. "You learn a lot from listening."

"Yeah, I can see that," Ash muttered under his breath. "Shit, we have more blips."

"I see them," Kella replied.

Ash decided right then and there that he was going to owe his grandma's memory a lot more apologies. His knuckles were almost white from his grip on the armrests. It had been a long time since he was in the passenger seat of an aircraft and he definitely didn't like it.

"Careful," he warned.

"I can do this, Ash," Kella reassured him.

It took everything in him not to crawl out of his seat when the freighter drifted closer to the wall of the narrow canyon. He pursed his lips to keep from saying anything that might distract Kella. Instead, he tried to think of some of the prayers he learned in Sunday school. Unfortunately, his mind was a blank. Well, not entirely blank – more like filled with every cuss word he ever learned in every language he could remember.

"Too narrow!"

The words slipped from his lips before he could bite them back. His startled hiss filled the cockpit when the freighter suddenly rotated. The sound of scraping followed by a loud explosion shook the ship.

"I told you… I know what I am doing," Kella replied.

Ash nodded and watched in fascination as she threaded her way through the canyon. The three blips went to two, then one. The last one hung on to their tail like a Rat Terrier to a squeaky toy – irritating and tenacious.

Actually, he was very proud of himself when he didn't release a squeak or two of his own. The first time was when Kella fired on a low-hanging rock cluster in an attempt to stop their pursuer. The second time was when they came upon the unexpected wreckage of a still smoldering spaceship which did not make it through the canyon. It was only Kella's quick reflexes that prevented them from becoming another one of the skeletal remains that already littered the area. The flying remains of burning metal that flew past them told Ash that the last blip wasn't as quick thinking.

"Finally! I thought he would never die," Kella muttered.

Ash melted back into his seat. He had to focus on each of his fingers individually to get them to relax their grip on the armrest. Wiggling his stiff digits, he lifted a hand and ran it down his face. He could see the end of the canyon up ahead. They shot out of it, skimming the low desert for several miles before she pulled back and the freighter cut a path upward through the atmosphere and into space.

"Where did you learn to fly like that?" Ash finally asked, turning to look at Kella.

She shot him a quick look. "The gaming programs at Tallei's bar. I used to play them when she wasn't looking," she said with a grin.

Ash gaped at her. He knew his mouth had to be hanging open, but he couldn't help it. Snapping it shut, he unstrapped his harness.

"Please tell me this thing has a bathroom. I think I need to clean my pants," he said.

Kella snorted. "Very funny. My freighter has two relief stations. The first is down the corridor. It is the last door on the left. The other is attached to the sleeping cabin. There is only one on board. I use the other cabin as storage," she explained before pausing. "Ash… I *really* did know what I was doing. The simulator games are very good. I know the programmer," she added with a smile.

"I'll remember that next time," he chuckled.

He pushed out of the seat. He hadn't really pissed in his pants, but she sure came close to scaring it out of him a couple of times. He walked down the steps and along the corridor until he reached the end where the bathroom was located.

It wasn't a large room, but it contained the two essential things he needed – a toilet and a sink. He relieved his bladder, then hunched over the sink, holding onto the sides. He closed his eyes and drew in deep, calming breaths until he felt like he was back in control. Waving his hand under the tap, he scooped the cold water in his hands and washed his face.

Looking up at the back wall, he stared at his reflection in the metal. He was on a spaceship… in space… with a beautiful alien woman who heated his blood… *and* they just outran the bad guys in a deadly canyon using skills Kella learned from an alien video game.

"God, I love this world!" Ash muttered and laughed deeply.

Chapter 18

"This system controls the hyperdrive. It will not operate unless you program a course in it that corresponds with an existing star map. If you try to override it, you could find yourself on a collision course with a star, asteroid, planet, or moon. There is a large amount of distance between space objects, but it is still possible to collide with one of them if you are not careful," Kella said.

Ash nodded. The physics of the universe were the same, no matter which part of it you were in. He was discovering that this section of it, wherever in the hell that was in the vast universe of star systems, learned how to traverse the vastness of space by using a combination of those laws of physics and technology. The technology of the gateway was incorporated into each spaceship, though on a much, much smaller scale. The larger the ship, the farther it could travel in a shorter period of time.

"This is my navigation system."

He turned his attention to the panel she was indicating. A puzzled frown creased his brow. Why did each panel look like it was built out of parts from a Radio Shack Black Friday Sale? Hell, it looked like there was duct tape around some of the edges.

"Why is everything so… patchworked?" Ash questioned with a wave of his hands at the console.

Kella sat back in her seat and scanned the console with a critical eye. He could see the defensive look that came into her eyes. She worried her bottom lip with her teeth for a second before she looked back at him.

"It took me many years to build this. I had to barter for parts or salvage them from the ship graveyard. I learned a great deal from some of Tallei's customers. I was not exaggerating when I said I knew every bolt on this freighter," she said.

Ash saw the self-doubt in her eyes and felt like kicking himself. This was one of the most ingenious alien space crafts he had ever been on. Of course, it was his only one, but that didn't matter to him. That Kella built something like this, which would have boggled even the greatest minds on Earth, was nothing short of incredible.

"I had help, of course," she added.

"I think it is awesome, Kella," Ash said, reaching out to touch her cheek.

Kella's expression cleared and she grinned. "I could show you the rest of it," she suggested.

"I was hoping you'd say that," Ash replied, pushing out of his chair.

He had been itching to do more exploring. He took a peek into some of the rooms on the way back to the cockpit from the bathroom, but the only thing that did was pique his interest even more. He stepped aside so Kella could pass. Unable to resist, he wrapped his arm around her waist and pulled her against him before brushing a kiss across her lips.

"Why did you do that?" she asked in surprise.

"Because I wanted to," he retorted.

She gazed up at him with a slight frown before she turned away with a smile. "You have my permission to do it again whenever you wish," she said with a regal wave of her hand.

A startled chuckle escaped Ash at her haughty tone. He watched her descend the short flight of steps. Was there just a little more sway to her hips than normal? he wondered. The grin on his face grew when she glanced over her shoulder at him with a mischievous, sexy glow in her eyes and what looked suspiciously like a smirk on her lips.

"Oh, darling, you probably shouldn't have said that. I have a lot of making up to do," Ash muttered under his breath.

..*

General Roan Landais stood looking out over the devastating results of Director Andronikos' orders. The once magnificent city of Jeslean's capital lay in ruins. Smoke rose from the destroyed remains of the buildings. More than a thousand years of architecture was laid to waste in just a few hours.

He knew about the brutality of his uncle and father. What remained of the headquarters of the Gallant Order stood out above the ruins. The center tower still stood overlooking the city. It was severely damaged. Large sections were missing and it was streaked with black from the soot of the fires burning around it.

Roan wondered how long it would take for his uncle or father to realize what they had done. The tower would be a symbolic beacon for the rebels. He had no doubt that the images of the lone tower, still standing sentinel over the wreckage, were already circulating around the star systems.

"Sir, your transport is ready," a soldier stated, coming to stand behind him.

"Excellent," Roan replied.

"Will you need anything else, General Landais?" the soldier asked.

"No, that will be all. You are dismissed," Roan replied.

"Yes, sir."

Roan heard the man click his heels together and saw the reflection of his salute, but ignored it. Instead, he continued to stare out at the tower. The rebels would use this to inspire their followers to the cause. The timing of this display of ruthless power could not have come at a worse time. He would have advised his uncle and father to wait, but the order was already in the process of being carried out before he was informed.

His meeting with the two most powerful men in the star systems demonstrated his need for caution and vigilance. He had no doubt that the drink his uncle poured for him at that meeting was poisoned. Over the years, he had plenty of time to study and analyze both men up close and personal. He could read them well.

Roan thought of the alien man he saw on his Battle Cruiser. The man was skilled in the art of warfare, but that didn't concern Roan. No, what concerned him was the mocking arrogance in the man's eyes when he shot Roan a two-fingered salute. The gesture was a gauntlet thrown down in challenge.

He ran through what he knew of the stranger. The information was limited. The wreckage of the spacecraft they found would take years to analyze. The capsule that was recovered revealed the man came from somewhere with an advanced technology. It didn't help matters that the capsule was damaged by a Tusku. The creature urinated all over it to mark its territory.

No, the most important knowledge came from the brief encounter he had with the man aboard the Battle Cruiser. The man brazenly walked onto his ship and freed a prisoner right from under his nose. His gaze narrowed in thought. How did the man come to have a Staff of the Gallant Order? Did he receive it from Jemar de Rola or was it already his?

In the end, even that would not be important. The overwhelming misconception held by his uncle and father was that power came from a show of physical force. That was what his uncle and father believed. Roan knew that true power came from something far less tangible – it came from hope. The arrival of the man and his friends would give the people that hope, and the image of the Ancient Knights of the Gallant's tower would symbolize their rallying cry.

Roan felt certain that the first awakening of the rebellion had already begun and the results would ripple across the stars to the far reaches of the known universe. The man who had boarded his Battle Cruiser and the ones who defeated Commander Jatur, were just the beginning.

He turned away from the large window and strode across the room. The Legion headquarters was one of the few buildings left unscathed. He took the lift down to the landing bay. Dozens of Legion fighters were taking off and landing. He boarded his personal fighter. A third signal was traced – and his personal sources assured him that the contents were still intact. It was time to discover if the legends which prophesied the return of the Ancient Knights were true.

Roan encrypted his flight coordinates. With a flick of his wrist, he enabled a jammer so that his ship could not be tracked. He did not want anyone – Legion or Gallant – to know where he was going.

Chapter 19

"You are beautiful," Ash murmured, threading his fingers through Kella's short hair.

"And you are going to give me a very big head if you continue to tell me that," Kella teased.

Ash chuckled when she leaned up to brush a kiss across his lips. His body should have been a pile of liquid mush from all the activities he and Kella enjoyed over the last couple of hours. Hell, he should probably be comatose! Instead, his body hummed with energy.

"What does this mean?" Ash asked, tracing the tattoo along her neck.

The teasing light in Kella's eyes faded and she pushed against him. He fell to the side, rolled, and bent his arm to rest his head on it. His gaze ran over Kella when she sat up. She tucked the top blanket around her and rose to her feet.

"It is the mark of a Turbinta. It defines who and what we are," she replied before walking across the room and disappearing into the bathroom.

"If it means beautiful, funny, intelligent, kick-ass, and totally hot, I think they got it right," he said in a soft tone.

He rolled onto his back and stared up at the ceiling. The tour of the ship didn't taken very long. There were basically two levels containing a dozen compartments. Most of them were used for storage or to house the mechanics of the ship. The three he was familiar with were the cockpit, the bathroom, and the cargo hold where they entered the ship. He soon discovered the lower section which contained the engine room and weapons array. This deck contained the galley, the captain's cabin with a private bath the size of a standard head on a sailboat, another cabin that was packed with supplies, and an assortment of electrical and mechanical rooms.

Ash turned his head and rolled onto his side when Kella reemerged from the bathroom. Her hair was damp and she had combed it back. She was also dressed in the familiar black uniform she appeared to prefer. Personally, he would love to see her in a little black dress with high heels.

"No," she said, shaking her head and walking toward the door.

"No what?" Ash asked, sitting up.

Kella paused in the doorway. "I see the look in your eyes, Ashton Haze. I'm hungry and I have work to do before we intercept Hutu Gomerant. Since I am unsure what our reception will be, I need to be prepared," she stated with a pointed look at his lap.

Ash glanced down and grimaced. She had taken the top blanket with her. All he had was the thin sheet and it was not doing much to cover the results of his current thoughts. He looked back up at her and grinned.

"I told you, I have a lot of time to make up for," he replied with a shrug.

"You… I will be in the galley. You have five minutes if you wish to eat," Kella retorted, turning away.

"Ten! Give me ten," he shouted behind her.

"Five!" she replied.

Ash stood by the bed. "Damn, but I think I'm in love with that woman," he chuckled.

..*

Five minutes later, Ash walked into the galley. Kella glanced at him in surprise. He grinned and wiggled his eyebrows at her. She rolled her eyes at him and turned back to what she was doing.

Ash sniffed the air. "That smells… interesting," he said, peering over her shoulder. "Is that even edible?"

"Yes," Kella replied, turning and holding out the gray glob in a small tray.

Ash hesitantly took it from her and lifted it to his nose. "When did it expire? Last century?" he asked in a wary tone.

Kella turned and leaned back against the counter. "If you don't want to eat it, go hungry. It was cheap and nutritious," she remarked, folding her arms.

"You mean that you actually paid someone for this?" he asked in disbelief.

Kella dropped her hands and reached for the tray. Ash jumped back several steps and grinned. She growled at him.

"If you don't want to eat, that is your decision. I do not waste food," she said.

"It's all good. I'm up for new experiences – as long as they don't kill me. Besides, I need food to rebuild my energy for later," he said, turning to walk over to the table.

"What is happening later?" she asked.

Ash slid onto the bench and wiggled his eyebrows again. "You, me, and some rock-n-roll, darling," he stated.

He picked up a utensil that looked suspiciously like a spork and took a bite of the food. The food was surprisingly flavorful considering its unappetizing color. He started to comment on it when his mouth suddenly ignited with a fire that burned a path all the way to his stomach. Tears filled his eyes and he desperately reached for the cup Kella placed on the table with her food. He tipped the cup and drained it in one long gulp.

Kella sat down across from him and shook her head. "You are a very strange man, Ashton Haze," she said, taking a big bite of her food.

"Holy shit that is hot," Ash croaked.

She paused and shrugged. "I've had hotter," she said.

He refilled the cup with water from a container she placed on the table earlier. Picking up a second cup, he filled it as well and sipped it until he felt like the lava he swallowed solidified. He sure hoped that Kella had other food on board or he might just starve.

"So, what is the plan?" he asked.

"Are you going to eat that?" she asked. Ash shook his head and pushed the tray toward her. She pulled the tray in front of her and began eating. "I need to check the systems. If we meet up with any Legion ships, I want to make sure that everything is in working order in case we have to run."

"How do you plan to contact Hutu?" he asked.

Kella shrugged. "It will be dangerous. The Legion will be monitoring communications. If we send or they receive, the transmission could be traced. There are many factors I need to consider. It will take almost three days to get to Tesla Terra. I can only hope that the Legion will take longer since they are moving more ships. The Battle Cruisers do not travel as quickly, and they will not want to risk leaving them unprotected," she said.

Ash bowed his head in frustration. He stared into his cup for several minutes. Everything she said was true. Hell, he had dealt with the same situations back home. Radio silence during a mission was vital when in enemy territory. He released a sigh and looked up at her.

"I guess the first task is to make sure this floating palace is in tip-top shape. I'm pretty good with a wrench if you'd like some help," he said.

Kella licked the last bit of food off of her spork and nodded. "I do not know which ship you are talking about, this is not a palace, but I could use the help. I need to work on the shields," she said.

"I'll take a look at the platform. It would be nice to be able to open and close it without having to beat the crap out of it," Ash said, picking up their dishes.

"What are you doing?" Kella asked.

Ash winked at her. "The dishes," he replied.

Kella watched him with her mouth hanging slightly open. He didn't mind doing the domestic stuff. His grandmother had a policy when he was growing up – whoever cooked didn't have to do the dishes. It was a great lesson in learning how to cook and how to clean. He placed the dishes in the small sink and began washing them. He started when he felt Kella's hands run down over his sides and around to the front.

"What are you doing" Ash asked, glancing over his shoulder at her.

"Turning the dish washer on?" she quipped.

"The switch is a little… yep, you found it," he replied.

"Ash," Kella murmured.

Ash heard the change in her voice. There was a slight note of confusion in it. He turned when she pulled her hands away and rubbed them down the sides of her pants.

"What is it?" he murmured, tilting her chin back with a damp finger.

"You confuse me," she replied.

He gazed down into her dark brown eyes and tenderly smiled. "If it helps, you do the same thing to me. We'll figure things out," he promised before bending to brush a kiss along her lips.

"There is also a dish cleaner next to the sink that cleans them without using water," she said with a small smile as she took a step back.

"Now she tells me," he muttered, watching Kella grin at him before she turned and walked out of the room.

He could tell that she didn't want to talk about what was happening between them – not yet. There were things she wasn't telling him. Natta tried to do so back on Torrian, but he let the other woman know that any discussion of his relationship with Kella was off-limits. Kella would tell him when she was ready.

Ash finished washing the dishes, found a cloth and dried them. It gave him time to think. This world was so different – yet, some things would always be the same, no matter where in the universe you were – plates, cups... the fight against dickheads who wanted to rule the world.

"I always did want to save the world," he murmured, storing the items in the drawer and cabinet before turning to look around the room. "And win the girl."

At that moment, Ash was certain of two things: he wanted Kella permanently in his life and he would fight to protect his new life here. He leaned back against the counter as those two realizations washed through him. It was the first one though that really shocked him.

The word permanent never entered into any relationship he had in the past. Hell, if it had, he would have been gone so fast the door wouldn't have had a chance to hit him in the ass on the way out. This time it was very different. This time, he wanted to see where their relationship went.

"Ash, I have tools if you need them," Kella said, stopping in the doorway to consider him.

He blinked, noticing she had two bags, one in each hand. Pushing away from the counter, he strode across the room and took one of them off her hands. He would have carried both of them for her if he thought he could get away with it. She shot him a quizzical look before she turned away.

Yes, this is my kind of woman, Ash thought, watching Kella stride down the corridor with a tool bag in her hand and a blaster on her hip.

Chapter 20

Two days later, Ash had a much better appreciation of alien technology. Kella's freighter might not be as shiny and new as the Gliese 581 had been, but it was far more complex and ingenious. He also had a great new respect for Kella's technical and mechanical skills.

Upgrading a freighter that could travel at speeds humans only dreamed about, with an effective weapons and defense system, was a lot different than rebuilding the 1969 Boss 429 Mustang that he bought while in high school. He and Josh spent most of their high school years working on the damn thing. They pooled every dime they earned to put it back together.

Glancing around the engine room of the freighter, he couldn't imagine how much it must have cost to buy and rebuild this thing. They were on their final section for repairs. He tore apart both hydraulics joints that operated the platform and rebuilt them. The seals were leaking and some of the gears were worn and needed replacing. Kella had a nice supply of spare parts on board and he was able to find what he needed to rebuild the side that was sticking.

After that, he repaired some of the lighting, worked on the environmental system when a heater coil shorted, and cursed up a storm while he watched Kella complete a six hour spacewalk to mount additional weapons. She grunted the word 'pirates' when he asked why a freighter needed laser cannons. When he had asked why she had so many knives and laser pistols hidden in every nook and cranny, she had growled at him not to touch them – that they were there for a reason. And she kissed him silly when he asked her what the name of her freighter was and told him he was driving her crazy with all his questions – but, there had been a twinkle in her eye that told him she was enjoying answering them.

"How are you doing?" Kella asked, leaning over the edge of the railing to look down at him.

Ash glanced up and smiled. "Almost done. This thing is humming," he replied.

"I am going to get cleaned up. After that, I will prepare some food for us," she said.

"Sounds good. I'll need about another ten minutes to clean up and store everything here," he responded, turning so his voice was partially muffled.

..*

Kella gazed down at Ash's back for a moment before she forced herself to turn away. He had stripped out of the Torrian tunic and was wearing a form-fitting black shirt. The front of it had a small emblem over his left pectoral.

She climbed the steps to the top level and walked down the corridor to the cockpit. She wanted to check their trajectory again. They were making better time than she had expected.

Climbing the short set of steps, she slid into the pilot's seat. Her stomach clenched when she saw that she had a message. Glancing over her shoulder, she returned her attention to the console and touched the communications screen. The screen flickered for a moment before she saw Tallei's familiar face.

"Kella, your time is running out. I have been following your progress and know that you have the Ancient Knight with you. There was a report that a Turbinta was involved in killing several Legion soldiers. I am disappointed that you were seen. That will be dealt with when you return. Do not be foolish, Kella; complete your mission. I told you, Turbintas must treasure nothing."

The transmission flickered again before cutting off. Kella raised a hand to touch the tattoo at her throat. Tallei's voice was a chilling reminder of who Kella was and what she was supposed to be doing. Her mentor's words sent a wave of unease through Kella.

She wasn't afraid of what would happen to her for being seen. Tallei would beat her, then send her through trial after trial until Kella remembered that she was nothing more than a ghost in the shadows – an assassin who must never feel the touch of the sun upon her face.

No, what caused the unease was Tallei's statement that she was following Kella's progress. The only way that Tallei could know where she was heading was if her mentor had placed a tracking device on the freighter. But, where? She and Ash had been over every section of the freighter. Where could Tallei have hidden a tracking device that would ….

"No!" Kella whispered.

She twisted out of the chair toward the corridor. Jumping past the stairs, she ran toward her cabin. She swung through the doorway, frantically scanning it. A slow anger burned inside her. Tearing open one storage cabinet after another, she ran her hands along the insides. When she didn't find anything there, she dropped to her knees and searched under the table and chairs.

"Where would you have hidden it, Tallei? Where would you think I would not look?" Kella whispered to herself.

The answer came to Kella like a blow to the gut. Swallowing, Kella crawled across the floor to the bed. She reached under it, feeling for the loose panel in the wall behind the headboard. Pulling it out, Kella felt around for the small box that she kept hidden in the wall. The small box with the few treasures she had collected over the years.

"No," Kella's strained cry echoed through the small room.

Her fingers closed around the tracking device. Tallei had found and taken her small box of treasures and left instead a reminder that Kella was still under her control. Kella scooted out from under the bed and pushed up into a sitting position. She glared down at the glowing red lights. Rage unlike anything she had ever felt before flooded her.

Rising to her feet, she walked into the bathroom. Kella placed the tracking device down on the edge of the sink. Pulling one of her blades from the sheath at her waist, she placed the tip on the seam and struck it hard with her palm over and over until the tip pierced the seal. Picking up the device, she held it firmly in her grasp and worked the blade in, moving it back and forth until the casing popped open.

She sliced through the wires, watching as the red lights flickered and then faded. Tallei would know what she had done – yet, Kella didn't care. Turning, she dropped the pieces into the latrine and flushed it.

It wasn't until a drop of red splattered on the basin of the latrine that she realized she cut one of her fingers. Kella watched the blood mix with the small amount of liquid in the basin. She drew in a shuddering breath.

Tallei will know I cannot complete the mission, she thought.

"Hey! What happened? You're bleeding," Ash's deep voice exclaimed behind her in concern.

The burning sensation Kella felt before returned, only this time it was different. It didn't stop when she blinked. The pressure continued and the burning intensified.

"I cut my finger," she whispered in a barely audible voice, lifting her hand to look at the blood dripping down.

Gentle hands turned her. One lifted to guide her hand over the sink. Chilly water rinsed the blood away before it was lifted again and a cloth was wrapped around it. Kella looked up when Ash used his other hand to tenderly stroke her damp cheek.

"It doesn't look too bad. A bandage and it should be fine," he promised.

"What... What is wrong with me? Why... Why is... water coming out of my eyes?" she asked.

Her eyelids lowered when he brushed his thumb across her cheek again. It didn't help. The moisture continued to pool in her eyes and overflow down her cheeks.

"Haven't you ever cried before?" Ash asked.

Kella shook her head. "No. I... Tallei said a Turbinta does not know how to cry," she replied.

"Well, you do and there is nothing wrong with it. My grandma told me that tears heal the soul and ease the pain by washing it away. She once said that if another man ever told me that men don't cry, I should punch him in the nose or kick him in the balls, and then ask him if men cry. I don't think she meant for me to take her quite so literally. I've only cried a few times in my life, but each time I felt better afterwards," he told her.

"What would make you cry – besides being punched in the nose or kicked in the balls?" Kella asked, rubbing her cheeks against the palm of his hand.

"The day Josh's dad was killed and the day my grandma died," he said, pulling her into his arms and holding her close.

Kella wrapped her arms around his waist and held him close. She rested her head against his chest.

The soft beat of his heart, the warmth of his body, and the strong arms wrapped around her made her feel loved and protected. Her arms tightened around him.

Tallei was right; loving someone did make you more vulnerable, but it could also make you more dangerous, she thought.

Kella knew that she would do anything to keep Ash safe from the Legion. She didn't care about the contract. She didn't care that to defy or fail meant her almost certain death. The only thing she cared about was keeping Ash safe.

Chapter 21

"Your assassin failed," Andri Andronikos stated in an unemotional voice.

"The time is not yet up," Tallei responded.

Andri turned to stare at the face on the screen. The scarred face of the Turbinta contractor stared back at him. The scars along her face and the cloudiness of her damaged eye added to the sense of menace he felt.

"What do you know?" he demanded.

"She has one of the men you seek," Tallei replied.

Andri's gaze narrowed. "One of the men?" he questioned.

Tallei bowed her head. "She was paid to retrieve one. If you wish for the other – the one who killed your men on Tesla Terra – it will require more credits," she responded.

He tightened his grip on the gloves in his hand. If he didn't need the Turbintas' services, he would have sent his Battle Cruisers to wipe out the traitorous species long ago. Unfortunately, their services had been required, despite the heavy price tag. They were instrumental in the deaths of many of the Gallant Knights and their families.

"Name your price, Turbinta, but make sure you deliver or I will be coming after you next," Andri stated.

"Your threats mean nothing to us, Director. Save them for those who have something worth losing. One hundred thousand credits. When it is delivered, I will be in touch again," Tallei stated.

"How do I know you are telling me the truth?" Andri demanded, leaning forward to glare at the screen.

"You don't," Tallei replied, ending the call.

Andri resisted the urge to place one of his fists through the screen. A knock on the outer door drew his attention and he straightened. A moment later, General Coleridge Landais stepped into the room.

"What did you discover?" Andri demanded as he studied his half-brother.

"A message was placed on one of our soldiers on Torrian while he was unconscious," Coleridge replied, walking over to pour himself a drink. He lifted the glass and stared at it for a moment before turning to look at his brother with a raised eyebrow. "Is it…?"

Andri sent his brother an annoyed shake of his head. Throwing his gloves on the desk, he moved to stand near the window. For several minutes, neither man spoke. Coleridge walked over to stand next to him. Below, fighters flew over the destroyed city, searching for and killing any survivors.

"We will build a new Jeslean, Andri," Coleridge murmured, lifting the glass to his lips.

"We will build a new Order on all the worlds," Andri replied in a harsh tone. "Tell me about the message."

Coleridge grimaced in distaste and turned away to walk over to the couch. He sat down and leaned back.

"You know about the incident several days ago," Coleridge began.

Andri impatiently waved his hand. "Yes, yes... That is why we ordered Roan here," he stated.

"There was another, this time involving another stranger," Coleridge informed his brother.

Andri turned to gaze at his brother. "Have we acquired the second capsule?" he asked.

Coleridge shook his head. "No. While the first stranger was rescuing Packu de Rola from Roan's Battle Cruiser, another one was seen in the marketplace on Torrian. Roan ordered a lockdown on the planet and all buildings and ships searched. A squadron encountered a strange male. His description matches the sighting reported by a farmer on the outskirts of the city," he explained.

"Get to the point, brother. I care nothing for a farmer's strange sighting or a squadron's search. How do they know this may be a second sighting and that the male may have come from the ship that broke apart?" Andri demanded.

"There was an emblem displayed on the outer portion of the ship. Our scientists were able to reassemble that section. That emblem is the same as the one on the patch the farmer gave the soldiers, when he described a man with dark brown skin who stole clothing and weapons from his storage building. The video placed on the soldier from the marketplace shows the second capsule and warns that the Ancient

Knights of the Gallant Order have returned. The soldiers in the marketplace encountered this stranger and he defeated eight of them with the help of a woman. Another team is still missing," Coleridge said.

Andri stared at his brother in silence. He turned, walked over to the bar, and poured himself a drink. His mind raced through the implications as he replaced the stopper on the bottle.

"The woman... What did she look like?" Andri curiously asked.

Coleridge was silent for a moment before he replied. "The soldier only had a brief glimpse of her, but he believed she wore the mark of a Turbinta," he said.

Andri's fingers tightened on the crystal stopper before he forced them to relax. The old assassin said that her pupil had one of the strange males from the capsules with her. The other alien that had rescued Packu de Rola would come for him once word spread the Legion had captured his comrade.

"A trap," Andri murmured.

"A trap?" Coleridge asked with a frown.

Andri turned and walked back toward his brother. "We will set a trap. Find the Turbinta assassin and you will find the second man from the strange ship. We will then use him as bait to draw out the other one," he said.

"What of the Turbinta?" Coleridge asked.

Andri lifted his drink to his lips, pausing to return his brother's gaze. "Kill her," he ordered.

"I will personally oversee the mission," Coleridge said, standing.

Andri drained half of his glass. "What of Roan?" he asked.

Coleridge paused. "You do not need to worry about him, Andri. I raised him. He will not betray us," he said.

Andri held Coleridge's gaze before he nodded and finished his drink.

"Find the Turbinta, kill her, and bring the stranger to me," Andri stated.

"I will leave immediately," Coleridge replied.

"Do not fail, Coleridge," Andri added before Coleridge opened the door.

Andri watched his brother bow his head in agreement, opened the door and stepped out. Walking over to the window again, he rolled the empty glass in his hand. He knew of the legend, the one that promised the return of the Ancient Knights of the Gallant Order, that prophesied the enemy's downfall would come when the Ancient Knights were allied with a betrayer. There was no way the Ancients could have foreseen his rise to power. Andri's eyes narrowed on the skeletal remains of the old temple of the Gallant Order. He would allow it to remain as a warning to any who dared to resist him.

Turning back to his desk, he placed the glass on the corner and sat down in the seat. With a few taps of his fingers, the image of the old Turbinta assassin reappeared. He was pleased to see she appeared annoyed.

"I will no longer require your services. Consider the contract void," he stated, ending the call before she could say anything.

..*

"You move like this," Ash said.

Kella relaxed her body while Ash moved her arms and feet into the proper positions. Her breath caught when he placed his hands on her hips and adjusted her body position. She bit back her sigh of exasperation. He had been endlessly teasing her since she demanded that he teach her more of the moves he called self-defense.

"Now try it," he instructed, stepping back.

They went through the sequence of moves slowly at first. He blocked her kick, then the punch she threw. She struck again. The more she practiced the individual moves, the more she began to understand what each move was for and how each related to the next. Balance was important. It was very similar to what she learned from Tallei, yet different. This balance allowed her to increase the power of her attack on a more spiritual level – something she never thought of before.

He also taught her about Kiai and Kage no kiai. She thought it fascinating that the sound of a voice could be used. Unlike the silent techniques Tallei taught her, Ash not only encouraged her to use sounds, but also to focus on the harmony the three sounds created and the feelings of self-assurance which helped her maintain a sense of inner calm.

"Ei!" Ash growled.

Kella warily jumped back, watching him. She raised her leg, stopping his kick, but not the strike of his arm. Her breath hissed out before she remembered that he told her it was better to be vocal, as it made the blow less painful.

She immediately moved forward. "Toh! Ya!" she shouted, moving in on him and forcing him back out of the area they marked off for their training in the loading bay of the ship.

"You are picking this up very quickly," Ash said with a grin.

"Did I hurt you?" she asked in concern when she saw him rubbing his chest.

Ash chuckled and shook his head. "I'm fine. You got a good punch in that last time. Remind me not to piss you off," he replied.

"I…," Kella started to say when the sound of an alert rang out. "We are approaching the outer rim of Tesla Terra's space. We should be able to relay a shortwave transmission to the planet. It is less likely to be picked up by the Legion because of the frequency."

"That's—" he cringed when a high-pitched alarm suddenly sounded. What was that?" Ash asked over the noise.

"The shields have been activated," Kella said, taking off down the corridor at a run.

Kella grabbed the railing and jumped up to the cockpit level. She sank down into the pilot's seat and swiveled around. Her fingers flashed over the console.

"What is it?" Ash asked, sitting down in the co-pilot's seat.

"We are too late. The Legion forces have already arrived. Ash, I need you to operate the weapons," Kella said, watching as fighters streamed out of the two Battle Cruisers.

"Holy shit," Ash muttered as he watched a large wave of fighters begin firing on the Legion's fighters as they exited the Battle Cruisers.

"That must be the rebels attacking," Kella said. "Fire at anything that comes at us. We need to…."

Both of them watched in horrified fascination as first one and then the second Battle Cruiser suddenly began to break apart. Kella felt as if time stood still while her brain processed what was happening. It was only when she saw the shockwave rippling through those unfortunate enough to be too close to the destruction that she realized the danger they were in as well.

"Full shields forward, reverse engines maximum thrust, brace for impact," she said with growing alarm as the magnitude of what was happening hit her.

Kella and Ash both grabbed for the straps on their seats. Trying to work them with one hand while operating the ship with the other, Kella cursed and slammed the controls for the thrusters into full reverse before grabbing both ends of the straps and snapping the buckle.

"Can you shoot some of the larger debris?" Kella asked.

"You got it. This will be like playing Space Invaders back home… just a little more meaningful and deadly," he replied.

Kella rerouted as much power as she could to the forward shields. Freighters were designed to handle some large impacts, but nothing of this magnitude. If that wasn't enough, there were a few Legion fighters who still weren't aware of what was going on with the Battle Cruisers. Two Legion fighters zeroed in on their freighter. Kella reached up and shut off the alarms. Red lights flashed all over the console in response to the shockwave barreling toward them.

"One and two," Ash said in a grim tone, firing on two large pieces of debris heading in their direction. "Tweedle Dee and Tweedle Dum are about to get a couple of torpedoes shoved up their tailpipe, or in this case, the shockwave of an exploding big ass Battle Cruiser."

The two must have just realized what was happening because they suddenly started to veer off in different directions. The shockwave hit both of them broadside. The force was great enough that they were both sent spinning out of control. The debris fragments from destroyed fighters and the Battle Cruisers sliced through the last two fighters like a hot knife through butter.

Kella held her breath before she remembered what Ash told her about releasing it to help reduce the pain from a punch. They were about to get a major punch. She just hoped her freighter could handle it.

"Brace for impact," she said, turning to look at Ash's face.

The moment before impact, all the air felt like it was being sucked out of the freighter. Kella actually felt her body being pulled forward before it was slammed back against her seat with enough force to stun her. Her gaze remained glued to Ash. The muscles in his arms strained as he continued to grip the controls to the weapons. He continued to fire even while they were momentarily lifted out of their seats as the first shockwave passed over them.

New warning alarms began to shriek. Kella could see the power shield gages dropping as a second and third shockwave battered their aircraft. Engine three shut down when it overheated and engine four went into safety mode, powering down, but not cutting off.

Several minutes passed before the massive turbulence stopped. All around them were floating pieces of debris. In the distance, Kella could see numerous fragments falling toward the planet. They glowed brightly as they entered the planet's atmosphere. Many would completely burn up long before they could reach the planet, but some of the largest pieces would not.

"Do you have any idea what the hell just happened?" Ash asked, sitting in his seat looking stunned.

"They – They blew up two of the Legion's Battle Cruisers," Kella replied in a low, shocked tone.

"It looks like they are taking care of any surviving stragglers. We need to let the Gallant Order know not to attack us," Ash said.

"Yes. I've had the communications off because we could be tracked that way," she admitted, not yet ready to fully disclose who was hunting her now.

"Gallant Order, this is freighter T573821 inbound to Tesla Terra, please hold your fire. I repeat, this is freighter T573821 en route to Tesla Terra," Kella said.

She frowned when the only answer was static. It was possible that the force of the shockwave damaged the communications system. It was also possible that it caused interference with all the communications systems in the area. Deciding to chance that it was obvious they were not part of the Legion forces, she used the thrusters to guide them slowly through the minefield of wreckage.

"Hold your fire. I don't want them to mistake us for one of the enemy," Kella ordered Ash.

Ash leaned forward. "Is there anything left?" he asked.

Kella didn't answer. Instead, she continued moving carefully through the debris and closer to the planet. Every once in a while she could hear the sound of scraping against the hull when a piece moved against the shielded nose.

"What is that?" Kella asked, frowning and sitting forward.

Ash studied it. It looked like some type of small transport. Sparks from the shuttle lit up the ghostly debris field.

"It looks like it is still intact," Ash said.

"Josh… Cassa… can you hear me?" a voice suddenly said over the communications system.

"Josh…," Kella whispered, her eyes widening.

"Phantom One, do you copy?" the same voice repeated.

"Fuck!" Ash exclaimed. "Try to reach them. Ask them what his last known position was."

Kella nodded and switched the communications system on again. "This is freighter T573821, please identify the missing vessel. We are in the debris field," she requested.

"Screw this. Hey man, this is Lt. Commander Ashton Haze of the United States Navy requesting information on Lt. Commander Joshua Manson's last known position and description of his spacecraft, over," Ash demanded.

"Who is this?" another voice demanded.

Ash leaned forward. "Commander Ashton Haze, United States Navy. I am requesting information on Commander Joshua Manson."

"You are the one he talked about. The one we were searching for back on Torrian," the voice stated.

Ash raised an eyebrow at Kella. "Is this Hutu? The son of a devious old blind man named Kubo?" Ash asked.

The sound of a chuckle echoed through the communications system before it faded and was replaced with a somber tone. "Yes. Josh and Cassa were aboard a Legion shuttle. They were heading away from the Battle Cruiser when it exploded. I fear they didn't make it," Hutu replied.

"Well, if it is a little gray box we might have found them," Ash replied.

"Their shuttle was seriously damaged. We will retrieve it and bring it on board the freighter," Kella replied.

"I'll meet up with you once you have retrieved the shuttle," Hutu stated.

Kella's mouth tightened. "Affirmative," she stated, unbuckling the straps holding her down.

"Where are you going?" Ash asked, unbuckling his own straps.

"I need you to guide the freighter closer. I will seal off the loading bay so we can winch the shuttle inside. It will be a tight fit, but it can handle it," she said.

"Wait a minute! How are you going to winch it in? Do you have like a tractor beam technology or something I haven't seen yet?" he demanded.

Kella looked at him with a confused expression before she shook her head. "I do not know what this tractor beam technology is. I need to attach two cables to the shuttle. If we damage the freighter, we risk dying. If we damage the shuttle, it could be enough to kill whoever is inside if they aren't already dead. The longer you keep me talking, the more likely it is this will be a waste of our time," she snapped.

Ash blinked in surprise at her tone. She glanced away. If Ash's friend was on that shuttle, she needed to do what she could to help him, even if her heart did feel like it was breaking.

Chapter 22

"Keep an open line of communication with me the entire time," Ash instructed.

"I will. Let me know once you are adjacent to the shuttle," Kella replied, adjusting the communications link and sealing the storage bay off from the rest of the ship.

Kella quickly suited up. She shouldered into the propulsion pack and attached a tether to the clip at her waist. She scanned the bay to make sure that everything was secured before she walked over and pulled down the manual override release for the platform. Once the light turned from red to green, Kella pressed the button to open the back platform. She reached up and pressed the upper section as well.

The magnetic boots she wore held her in place while the section decompressed. Glancing up, Kella could see pieces of debris floating by. She would have to be very careful. If a piece hit her, it could propel her away. If it cut through her tether, she would only have the propulsion pack to help her get back to the freighter. If it tore her suit, she would die. The freighter's shields could only provide her with limited protection.

"We're coming around," Ash warned.

"I see it. Thirty degrees to your left… twenty… ten… five… four… three… hold," Kella instructed. "I'm going out."

Bending, Kella picked up the large, magnetic tethers in her hand. She walked to the end of the platform before deactivating her boots and kicking off in the direction of the shuttle. She breathed in and out evenly and kept her gaze fixed on the shuttle.

Out of the corner of her eye, she saw a large section of a fighter heading toward her. She released the two thick tow lines and gripped the handles of the propulsion pack. She barely had time to avoid a collision.

"Damn it, Kella, please be careful," Ash's strained voice echoed in her ear.

"I will," she promised, realizing he could probably see everything from the security feeds.

She retrieved the tow lines and refocused on the shuttle. From the damage she could see outside, she would be amazed if the environmental system was still working. She extended her arm to slow her forward momentum as she neared the shuttle.

"I'll need to attach a tether to the near side, then have you guide the freighter around to the other side so I can attach the second tether," Kella said.

"Roger, that. Turning to the Port side on your mark," Ash repeated.

Kella chuckled. "You are much better at this than I realized," she teased.

"I may have had a year or twenty of training," he retorted.

"The first tether is attached. Bring the freighter around on my mark," Kella said. "Now."

..*

Ash could feel the tension in his shoulders. The area was a drifting minefield and Kella was in the middle of it. Nothing about the situation was giving him a good feeling. If he had his way, he would be the one out there.

"I'm attaching the second tether now. I can see inside. I see a man and a woman. Neither are conscious. I don't know if they are alive or not," Kella said.

"Let me know when I can activate the winch," Ash replied.

"I'm clear. Activate winch," Kella instructed.

Ash reached over and set the winch in motion. He felt the freighter jerk as the dead weight stretched the tethers taut before the craft was slowly pulled in. He adjusted the thrust to compensate. Engine three was still offline and engine four was still not at full capacity. He kept it steady, watching the view screen as the shuttle drew closer.

"Ash, there is a large section of debris heading for the tow lines hauling the shuttle," Kella's voice warned.

He glanced around trying to get a visual but he couldn't see anything from this angle. He switched the screen's view. A low curse escaped him. A large section of what looked like part of a Battle Cruiser was spinning toward them end over end.

"Are you clear?" he demanded.

"If it strikes the tethers or the shuttle, we will lose them," she said.

"I repeat, are you clear?" Ash demanded.

"I… Yes, I'm clear," Kella replied in a barely audible voice.

Ash pressed the thrust control down on the freighter. He wasn't going to lose Josh and he wasn't going to lose Kella. The freighter slowly pushed forward. He mentally calculated how much time he had. It would be close.

"Come on… come on…. Just a little more," Ash muttered under his breath.

He swallowed, watching the distance narrowing until the huge chunk of debris passed by, only a small section knocking against the back of the shuttle before continuing on its course and disappearing. Ash's gaze frantically searched the screen. Where was Kella?

"Kella…," Ash called out.

"I'm here," she said.

It took a moment for him to spot her clinging to the side of the shuttle. A wave of weakness washed through him. If he had misjudged the position by less than a meter, he would have lost everything he cared about.

"We need to have a talk when you get back on board," he swore.

"I know," she replied, a slight wobble in her voice. "We are coming in now. I'll pressurize the cargo bay as soon as it is safe to do so."

Ash slowly guided the freighter out of the heaviest concentration of the debris field. His jaw ached from grinding his teeth. There was nothing he wanted more than to check on Kella and Josh, but he couldn't – yet.

"Pressurizing now," Kella said.

Ash watched the light change from red to green. The moment it was safe, he rose out of the pilot seat and jumped down the steps to the corridor. He strode down the corridor, reaching the end at the same time Kella opened the seal between the two sections.

"Ash—" Kella started to say before her words were cut off.

Ash captured Kella's lips and pulled her roughly against his body. He bent, tightening one arm around her waist while cupping her ass with the other to lift her off the floor. Turning, he pressed her against the wall of the corridor and deepened the kiss for a moment before he released her.

"Don't you ever scare the hell out of me like that again," he murmured in a rough voice.

Kella touched his cheek as he lowered her back to the floor. She turned to look at the shuttle. It looked worse in the lighting of the bay.

"We need to check on your friend," she said in a voice that held a slight tremble.

Ash drew in a deep breath and released her. He stepped into the cargo bay and walked over to the shuttle. He wasn't sure how to open the damn thing.

"Stand aside," Kella warned.

He watched as she pried open a panel with the tip of her knife. Within seconds, she had the outer door open. She glanced at him before stepping through the doorway.

Lights flashed in warning and sparks rained down from many of the instrument panels. Lying on the floor just inside the doorway was Cassa de Rola. Blood coated a spot at her temple and along one arm.

The woman groaned softly and pushed up only to collapse again. Kella hurried to her and knelt down by her side. Ash bent down next to her. Kella glanced through the opening. The man who must be Ash's friend sat strapped in the chair. His eyes were closed, blood ran down along his neck, but she could see his chest moving.

"Help me get her to our cabin. I will take care of her there while you help Josh," Kella said.

Ash's face paled and his eyes widened. "Aw hell, Josh," he muttered, taking in his condition.

Kella reached out and touched his arm. "He lives. Help me with the woman," she requested again.

Ash nodded, helping Kella check the woman for broken bones before he carefully picked her up. He exited the shuttle and strode down the corridor to their cabin, then carefully laid the woman down on the bed.

Kella stood in the doorway. There was an expression on her face that he hadn't seen before – as if she were sad… and scared. He paused and ran his fingers down along her cheek. She tilted her head back.

"Are you okay?" he asked.

Kella nodded. "Go check on your friend. I will care for the woman," she said.

Ash gazed down at her for a moment before he nodded. He must have been mistaken. If anything, the expression in Kella's eyes reminded him of the way she looked back in the alley the first night they met.

Striding down the corridor, apprehension and excitement built inside him. He wasn't alone. Josh survived, which meant there was still a chance that the others did as well. Crossing the cargo bay, he disappeared back inside the shuttle.

Chapter 23

"You're a Turbinta," Cassa de Rola said, warily watching Kella.

"Yes."

"Are you going to kill us?" the woman demanded in an exhausted voice.

Kella wrung out the warm, damp cloth and held it up. "I would not be cleaning the blood off of you if I was going to draw more," she pointed out.

"What is your name?" Cassa asked.

Kella shrugged. "Kella," she replied.

Cassa frowned and looked around the room. She tried to sit up, but fell back against the pillows with a soft moan. Her hand trembled when she raised it to her head.

"Where am I? Josh? Is… is he…?" Cassa asked, reaching for Kella's hand.

Kella was surprised at the strength of the woman's grip. She stared down at Cassa de Rola. For some reason, she thought the woman was younger than she was. Kella gently pulled Cassa's hand back down to the bed and worked her fingers free.

"He lives. Ash is with him," Kella replied in a stiff voice.

"Ash! Josh's friend… How?" Cassa murmured in shock.

"If I tell you, will you lay still so I can see what type of injuries you have?" Kella finally bit out in frustration.

Cassa nodded. Kella gently wiped the blood away from the scrape to Cassa's forehead. It was minor, more of a rash burn. Head wounds tended to bleed a lot, but healed quickly. Kella turned her attention to Cassa's arm. There was a significant amount of blood there. Kella gripped Cassa's sleeve and ripped it open.

"I met Ash on Torrian. He learned that Josh was still alive. We tried to find you there, but we were too late. Kubo, Hutu's father, learned of the Legion's destruction of the cities on Jeslean and their intentions to destroy those on Tesla Terra as well. The Legion locked down Torrian after I fought with Josh in the warehouse, but we were able to escape. We came to warn Hutu of the attack, but we were too late. We arrived as the two Battle Cruisers exploded. We saw the shuttle, realized it was you, and I attached tethers to it while Ash pulled the shuttle in. This is my freighter and I am a Turbinta. Now, you know everything," Kella said, cleaning the wound and wrapping it. "Your arm is cut, but not too deeply. Your head is fine, but may hurt. Do you feel pain anywhere else?"

Cassa winced when she sat up. "Everywhere?" she retorted with a wry smile. "Thank you for your help, but I'd really like to see Josh."

Cassa tried to stand up, but her legs refused to support her. Kella caught her and pushed an unresisting Cassa back down onto the bed, then propped the pillows under the woman's head. She stepped back and grimaced.

"If you promise not to move, I will see if he has regained consciousness and get Ash to bring him to you," Kella reluctantly promised.

Cassa nodded and closed her eyes. "I will remain here," she murmured.

Kella gazed down at Cassa for a moment before she turned. A dark scowl creased her brow when she saw a huge figure in the doorway. It was not that of Ash or the other man's. It could be none other than…

"Hutu Gomerant?" Kella asked, placing her hands on her hips.

"General Hutu Gomerant," the man replied.

"Watch her. She is still weak," Kella ordered.

Hutu raised an eyebrow at her. "I would watch your tone, Turbinta. I've cut the tongues out of those with less attitude," he warned.

Kella looked Hutu up and down before she shrugged. "You are bigger than Kubo. Did you take after your mother?" she taunted.

Hutu returned her gaze. Kella fingered the knife at her back. She was surprised when the large man laughed deeply, his lips curved in amusement. For a moment, she thought she was seeing a younger version of Kubo.

"I will watch Cassa, Little Fire Tongue, while you check on Josh," Hutu said, stepping to the side.

Kella dropped her arms to her sides and brushed past Hutu. She could feel the Torrian General's eyes burning a hole through her back. Straightening her shoulders, she couldn't help but overhear Cassa's voice when she spoke to Hutu.

"Hutu, do you think it is safe to trust her?" Cassa asked.

..*

"Josh! Dude, wake up! Hey, man, are you still alive?" Ash asked, gripping each side of Josh's face and turning it back and forth.

He had unstrapped Josh and lowered him to the floor. From the feel of Josh's pulse, it didn't feel like there was anything life-threatening to worry about. He also checked Josh's pupils and they looked normal. A happy sigh of relief washed through him when Josh lifted his hand and tried to shove him away.

"Turn… off… the… damn… spotlight," Josh croaked out. "Cassa…."

Ash chuckled in relief. Cussing was good. It meant Josh's brain wasn't scrambled.

"She's okay. Kella is with her," Ash replied. "Damn, but you are a sight for sore eyes."

Ash grinned when Josh groaned. He bent forward to check the cut on Josh's forehead again. It had finally stopped bleeding. It would serve Josh right if the first thing he saw was Ash's big ugly mug. It would be payback for scaring the shit out of him. Ash's grin grew when he was rewarded with a dark scowl.

"I swear if you kiss me, I'll knock the shit out of you," Josh threatened.

Ash couldn't contain the loud laugh that escaped him. It felt good to hear his best friend's voice again. Ash bent forward and wrapped his arm around Josh's shoulders to help him sit up. Josh winced and grunted before he rested his arms on his knees.

Ash rested his hand on Josh's shoulder. He was almost afraid to move it in case Josh disappeared. His throat tightened with emotion. It felt good to know he wasn't the only human anymore.

"You know, I could almost do it," Ash reflected in a quiet voice.

He twisted around and sat down next to Josh. He stretched his legs out and rested his hands on his thighs as he stared at the inside of the shuttle with a critical eye. The random thought crossed through Ash's mind that Josh was doing pretty good if he was flying something like this up into an enemy Battle Cruiser.

Ash could feel Josh's gaze on his face. A wry smile curved his lips. Josh was looking at him with an expression that told Ash that Josh was having a hard time processing the fact that they were both alive.

Josh finally shook his head and smiled. "The only thing you're missing is the hat and you could be Harrison Ford… with one hell-of a tan, that is. What could you almost do?" he asked in a scratchy voice.

Ash leaned back and drew his knees up. "Kiss you. I thought I was the only one alive."

"I thought the same thing. When I heard there was another capsule… and found out it was yours…." Josh released a deep breath and he glanced around the damaged shuttle. "Where are we?"

Ash was about to reply when he heard Kella's familiar footsteps. He glanced over his shoulder and smiled. His head jerked around in surprise when he heard Josh's harsh curse.

Kella stood in the doorway of the cockpit and dispassionately stared down at Josh. "Greetings, Joshua Manson," she said in a tone that could freeze a man's balls on a hot summer day.

Ash rose at the same time as Josh. He jerked in surprise when he saw Josh reach for the weapon at his side. Kella recognized what was happening and warily stepped back. Even as she did, Ash saw her hand move to one of the blades she always carried.

Ash held an arm out to Josh even as he protectively stepped in front of Kella. "Hey, Josh, whoa. Kella's alright. She's cool, man," he warned.

Josh shook his head and glared at Kella. "Cool?! She tried to kill us! She's a Turbinta assassin," Josh growled, staggering back a step.

Ash frowned in confusion. "Kella? An assassin? Naw, she's a freighter pilot. She saved my life," Ash insisted.

Josh shoved Ash to the side. "No. She tried to kill me in the warehouse. We fought and I knocked her out. Hutu was going to kill her, but I stopped him. I shouldn't have. What in the hell is she doing here?" Josh snarled.

Ash ran his hand down his face and looked back and forth between Kella and Josh. They warily eyed each other. Kella fingered the handle of her blades, but didn't draw them. Josh gripped a Staff that looked just like the one Kubo gave him. Things were seriously going south.

"Listen, you must be mistaken! Tell him, Kella. Tell him that you didn't try to kill him," Ash said, waving a hand at Josh.

Ash saw a look of resignation enter Kella's eyes. Her bottom lip trembled before she pressed it into a tight line. She shrugged her shoulders.

"Yes, I did. That was what I was ordered to do," she replied in a quiet voice.

Ash breathed out a sigh of relief. "See, she...." It took a few seconds for what she said to process. He turned to glare at her in disbelief. "What? Are you nuts? You can't kill my friend!"

Kella's body stiffened. "It was what I was paid to do; or at least, I would have been paid to do if I had been successful. I came to tell you that the woman wants to see him," she retorted in a defensive tone before she turned sharply on her heel and strode back out of the shuttle.

Ash stared after Kella in disbelief. Surely he must have missed something critical – like forgetting to tell him that she was an assassin sent to kill Josh. How the hell did someone forget to mention that?

The sound of Josh sinking down into the pilot's seat drew Ash's attention. Josh looked wiped out.

Josh's question was one he would like to have answered, too.

"Would you mind telling me what is going on?" Josh asked.

Ash folded his arms across his chest and leaned back against the wall. He gazed moodily at his friend. He wasn't sure what was going to happen next, but part of it was going to involve a very long, detailed discussion with Kella.

"Dude, if you don't know, how the hell am I supposed to? Remember? You are the one who always knows the answer to things, Sherlock. I'm just your wingman. This is one crazy, messed up world," he muttered.

..*

Several hours later, Ash was in a foul mood. Kella was avoiding him as much as possible. She worked on the engines, made sure the shuttle in the cargo bay was secured, and even did the laundry, stripping their bed and washing all the covers before remaking it.

At the moment, she and Hutu were having a staring contest. Ash was sure they would be counting out paces in the corridor any minute. If that wasn't enough, he thought he had broken through her wall, but she rebuilt it with re-enforced steel, keeping him at a distance again. Then, to top off the salt in the wound, Josh and Cassa were gazing at each other with lovey-dovey eyes.

Ash shot Josh an exasperated glare. "If you two keep staring at each other like that, I'm going to send both of you to a corner," he finally snapped in irritation.

He absently listened while Hutu explained what happened in greater detail. From the sound of the operation, it was a huge success. But with that success, there would come consequences.

"What now?" Josh asked. "How will the Legion respond, do you think?"

"The repercussions of the battle have already been felt across the galaxy…" Hutu said.

Ash absently listened as Hutu explained about the Legion Director's paranoia and how General Landais, aka Count Landais, had disappeared. He jolted back to attention when he heard Hutu mention that Landais may be tracking another emergency pod.

"… It is believed he is searching for another signal," Hutu explained.

Kella glanced around the table before her gaze paused on Ash's hard face. "There were two more. I picked up information about two more signals from another pilot I know. He said the Legion has posted a reward for the recovery of any capsules. He doesn't want anything to do with the Legion, but thought I might be interested since I knew the area the signals were last traced to," she murmured.

She turned to look at Josh when he leaned forward. "Are they the same signals that Landais is hunting for?" he asked.

"No. The last sighting of Landais was in the opposite direction. These… They were headed toward Turbinta. It won't take long for others to realize what the signals are. As I said before, the Director has promised a large reward for the contents of the containers – dead or alive," Kella said.

"We have to find them," Hutu retorted, rising up out of his seat.

Ash hid his grin when Kella shot the huge red man a defiant glare. He didn't miss the flash of fear or Kella's slight wince when the man suddenly stood up. Hell, he was hyper-aware of everything about her at the moment.

Kella shook her head. "If you went there, every assassin on the planet would be after you. The Director has placed a very high bounty on all of your heads," she said in a sharp tone.

"What do you expect us to do? Ignore the signals? Leave them to be discovered and used by the Director?" Hutu demanded.

"We go in after them regardless of the danger," Josh stated.

"And I'm telling you that you can't. You won't be successful," Kella reiterated.

"We can't just leave them," Ash said in frustration.

Ash saw Kella turn to look at him. There was an expression of resignation in her eyes. She searched his face before she spoke. Her expression softened and he could see the determination in her eyes.

"I never said that you should," Kella murmured.

Chapter 24

"Are you going to continue to avoid me or are we going to talk about this?" Ash asked, leaning against a metal support beam in the engine room.

"If I ignore you, will you go away?" she asked, not turning to look at him.

"That is kind of hard to do in a small, enclosed space," he drawled in a dry tone. "Why didn't you tell me, Kella?"

"Tell you what? That I am a Turbinta? You knew that," she replied.

"You know that isn't what I'm talking about. You took advantage of my lack of knowledge," he retorted.

Kella didn't answer him right away. He watched her pick through the assortment of tools she laid out before picking up a curved pair of pliers. He folded his arms, not giving in to her desire for him to give up and leave her alone.

"I didn't want you to look at me the way others did," she finally admitted with a sniff. "You looked at me differently. You didn't see… You didn't see a killer, an assassin, someone who…."

Ash heard the tremble in her voice and straightened silently to step closer to her. He squatted down next to her and ran his hand along her shoulder. A shudder went through her and she sniffed again.

"I didn't look at you like someone who… what?" he asked in a gentle tone.

Kella bowed her head. He couldn't see her face. Her hair fell forward to hide it and she was turned away from him.

"You didn't look at me like I was the lowest life form in the star system," she answered, her voice barely audible above the hum of the engines.

"Kella…," Ash murmured, reaching out to touch her face.

She jerked away from him and stood up, still keeping her back to him. Her back was stiff, but he saw her raise her arm to brush it across her face. It took him a moment to understand why she was refusing to look at him.

"Are your eyes leaking again?" he asked in a slightly teasing tone.

Kella nodded. "Ye… Yes," she sniffed.

"I know how to make them stop," he said.

She turned her face toward her left shoulder as if to look at him, but she didn't. From this angle, though, he could still see her face. Her body shook when she drew in a deep breath before speaking.

"How?" she quietly asked.

Ash stepped up behind her and slid his hands along her hips. She slowly turned in his arms. Her head was still bowed and she looked at his chest instead of his face.

He drew her into his arms. "A hug, a kiss, and letting you know that I still think you are the most beautiful woman in the stars," he said, cradling her against him.

She sobbed softly and buried her face in his shirt. She wrapped her arms around his waist and held on so tight that he was surprised he could still breathe. Her body shook with her sobs. Realizing this was a new experience for her, he held her until she finally grew quiet.

She sniffed loudly. "I don't understand," she murmured in a voice still thick with tears.

Ash rubbed his cheek against her hair. "What don't you understand?" he asked.

Kella tilted her head back and gazed up at him. "Why do you not hate me?" she asked with a searching look.

Ash returned her gaze. He lifted his hand and smoothed his fingers along her flushed cheek. The look in her eyes was heartbreaking. It was obvious to him that she fully expected him to hate her now that he understood what a Turbinta was.

"Why would I hate you for being you? You're the woman I fell in love with – just because you are a Turbinta doesn't change my feelings. I'll admit that I hope this means you'll retire from that lifestyle, but I can't complain. Hell, I've got my own personal protection unit," he teased.

Kella searched his face. "You are a very, very strange man, Ashton Haze," she murmured.

Ash grinned down at her. "Yeah, but just remember – I'm your strange man," he retorted with a wink before he brushed a kiss against her lips.

"I will remember," she said.

Ash glanced at the engines. "So, what is the plan? Are engines three and four operational now?" he asked, nodding to the large cylinder.

Kella smiled and pulled out of his arms. "Yes, a couple of the circuit boards needed to be repaired. I want to keep the Legion shuttle. It might come in handy. I could use your help repairing it," she said.

Ash bent and helped her stow the tools. "Sounds good. So, what is the plan for your planet?" he asked.

Kella paused. "Find the other capsules, hopefully your friends, and get out alive," she replied, turning and walking over to the cabinet where she stored the tools.

Ash watched her for a moment before he shook his head. "Nothing like keeping to a simple plan of attack," he muttered.

Chapter 25

There was one thing Ash could say about the Turbinta home world – it looked depressing. It was a gray planet from afar and it looked even darker gray closer up. It wasn't until they were closer that he realized the gray swirling clouds were storms.

"It rains all but a few days each year," Kella commented, staring down at the world where she grew up. It looked nothing like the one she sometimes dreamed about. "Even the trees are gray."

"Lovely. No wonder people grow up there wanting to become killers. You know they have sun lamps for those who could use light therapy. It works wonders," he replied sarcastically.

"Not everyone wants to be a killer, Ash. We do so out of survival. There are clans on Turbinta. Each clan competes against the others to provide the most skilled assassins," Kella explained, looking at the world where she was raised through different eyes.

"What happens to those who don't make the cut?" he asked.

"If they demonstrate a useful skill, they might be spared. If they don't, they are either left to die or used as a target for training," she explained. "I was fortunate. I had both the skills and the ability to be a good assassin. Tallei was very pleased with my abilities."

Ash glanced at her. "But…."

Her lips curved in a rueful smile. "But, I was curious. I loved listening to the customers at Tallei's bar. She tried to keep me away from them, but it was impossible. She needed my help and I wanted the knowledge they could give me that she refused to share. And I…valued…certain things. I thought I hid that weakness well…but she knew. Still, I excelled in the training and I did what I had to in order to survive. If I had not killed my opponents, they would have killed me," she said.

"That is one messed-up world," Ash stated.

Kella shot him an amused look. "You have no idea," she teased.

"Do you have a reading on the emergency pods?" Ash asked.

"Yes, we will locate the one nearest to us first. It is in the Black Canyon region. It will be dangerous. The canyons are deep and slippery. There are narrow footpaths through them, but they often collapse due to the constant rain. If you fall in the river, you are dead. The runoff from the upper elevations keeps the river's water level high and fast flowing. The people live in cities carved into the cliffs, much like the Torrians do. It is difficult to see them because they build them behind the massive waterfalls created from the rain," she explained.

"Is there anything good about this place?" he asked in disbelief.

Kella thought for a moment and shook her head. "No, not that I am aware of," she replied.

Ash didn't comment. What the hell could he say? Sounds like the perfect vacation retreat – if you like visiting hell?

Two hours later, Ash decided that this was definitely the way hell would look in real life. His fingers gripped the controls as they cut through the lower atmosphere. Lightning flashed, illuminating tall, black spiraling peaks rising out of dark, ominous canyons. Rivers of water ran off the flat surface above and disappeared into the abyss.

"Where in the hell are we supposed to land?" he asked.

"Over there," Kella said, nodding to a high plateau.

"Oh, shit," Ash muttered under his breath.

The area Kella was pointing to was long and flat. The plateau was also very narrow at the base, looking more like a table balanced on a needle. Ash shook his head in wonder. He really hoped to hell that Kella knew what she was doing.

There was a strong crosswind. She came in low along the flat surface before rising up at the last second. Glancing out the front windows, Ash could see the water running through gouges along the surface like rivers. Kella turned so that she was heading into the wind and used the strong current of air to push the freighter back a little to the center of the plateau before she touched down. If she had tried to come in any other way, there was a chance wind would cause the freighter to shift and she would have missed the limited landing space.

"We will need to hurry. The stormy weather is worsening and the waters will rise. The signal is still strong and not moving, which is good. It means it is not in the river. I will need to set the security system. This area is not safe. I do not expect anyone to be here, but I do not want to take a chance on returning only to find the freighter gone," she said, shutting down the engines.

After unstrapping, they both exited the cockpit. Kella stepped into their room and began picking up the weapons she laid out earlier and concealing them on her body. She picked up a laser pistol, checked it and held it out to Ash.

"You may need this. Shoot anything that comes at you," she instructed.

He looked up at her startled. "What if it is friendly?" he asked, reaching for the gun.

"Trust me, it won't be," she replied. "Do you know how to use that?" she asked quietly.

Ash glanced down at the Staff Kubo gave him. He ran his fingers over the carvings before he added it to the belt Kubo also gave him to carry it. He picked up the belt and wrapped it around his waist.

"I know how to use it," he promised.

"When we go outside, follow me carefully. The rocks will be slippery and some of them are loose and will slide if you are not careful. The water erodes them," she instructed.

"How will we get down to the bottom?" he asked, glancing at her.

"Very carefully," she retorted with a wry grin. "We will not need to go all the way down. The signal I picked up is about two kilometers north of here."

"Great! Just a walk in the park," Ash replied.

Kella stopped and stared at him for a moment. "This is not a park like we saw at Kubo's residence, Ash. This is dangerous," she warned in a serious voice.

Ash chuckled, leaned forward, and brushed a kiss across her lips. Sometimes she took the things he said very literally. It was times like those that reminded him that he was in an alien world – not that everything else didn't help.

"I know," he said.

Minutes later, he was staring out at a very hostile, alien world. They had slipped on weather protective suits and helmets. Kella told him that the suits would keep them warm and dry from the icy wind and rain. The helmets allowed them to communicate and shield them from the driving rain so they could see where they were going.

"You don't want to walk off the cliff," she said, her voice echoing clearly in his ear.

Ash walked down the platform after her, bending forward when the wind threatened to knock him off. Once they exited the ship, Kella held up a remote and touched in a command. The platform rose without any issues, sealing the freighter.

"Now what?" Ash asked, turning to look across the landscape.

"Now we hope we don't die," she said, turning to begin walking up the steep incline.

..*

It took over two hours to reach the location where the signal was the strongest. The wind and rain had picked up for a brief time, almost blinding them. At one point, Kella insisted that they wait for it to pass. They sought shelter under a low outcropping of rocks. Fortunately, it didn't last long.

"The weather helps keep other worlds from attacking us," Kella murmured, staring out at the rain. "I once overheard a customer of Tallei's say the pirates had a bet going on how long it would take for everyone on this planet to drown."

Ash chuckled. "I can understand why," he said.

Kella shook her head. "He would have been better off betting on how long a person would survive on Turbinta at all. The foolish man tried to argue with Tallei about paying for his bill," she murmured, pausing to turn to look at Ash. "She killed him."

"Ouch," Ash replied. "It looks like it is slowing down."

Kella nodded. She stepped out on the rock, turning when she heard a low rumble. Her eyes widened when she saw a wall of water heading toward them. Twisting around, she placed her hands in the center of Ash's chest and pushed him back.

"Flash flood!" Kella cried out, pushing them both as far as she could under the rock.

Kella felt Ash's arms wrap around her and he braced his feet. The wall of water hit the slanted rock, engulfing them on three sides. The sound of it was deafening. Kella pressed her body against Ash.

The water rose and flooded the black rocks. It swirled greedily around their legs, trying to suck their feet out from under them and plunge them into the rapidly flowing water. Kella felt her feet lifting up and she frantically grabbed for a section of rock behind Ash. Her fear of losing her footing and pulling Ash with her overriding everything else. His arms tightened around her, holding her against him.

"Hold on to me," he ordered.

"I won't drag you with me," she said, digging her fingers into a small crevice and hoping it didn't give way.

They clung like that for what felt like hours, but was actually mere minutes. As fast as the waters rose, they disappeared. Kella felt the water receding from around her feet and she once again had a firm footing.

"I've decided I don't like this place very much," Ash stated, slowly releasing her.

Kella released a choked laugh. "It isn't my favorite place either," she admitted, turning and attempting to leave the rock again. "Clear."

Ash jumped down off the rock and reached up to help Kella down. He winked at her when she looked at him in surprise. They both moved toward the edge of the cliff.

"There it is!" Ash exclaimed.

He pointed down to a long, rectangular box sitting precariously on a small shelf extending from the rocks several meters from where they were standing. It was hard to see if there was anyone inside. Large rocks covered the top, probably washed down from a previous flash flood.

"Let's go," she said, shrugging off her backpack. She walked over and knelt down. "I will go down and check the capsule."

Ash placed his hand over hers and shook his head. "No, I will. If anyone is in there and they are alive, I can lift them," he said.

Kella wanted to argue, but she knew he was right. She nodded and pulled the harness and hoist out before she stood and helped fit it onto Ash. She connected the buckles and pulled a short section of cable out of the front.

"Up, down, start, stop, emergency release. Do you understand? This will anchor you to the top. But be careful. There could be another flash flood. If there is, the water will be the least of your worries. The rocks that come with it are sharp and moving quickly and with enough force that they can pierce the helmets. I will keep an eye out and warn you. I… Ash…." Kella stared up at him. "Be careful… please."

"Careful is my middle name," he replied with a wink.

"Really? You have another name?" Kella asked in surprise.

Ash's chuckle told her that he was just teasing her again. She scowled and walked closer to the edge.

Turning, she counted three large steps in, aimed what looked like a miniature harpoon at the ground, and fired. She motioned for him to come closer. Leaning down, she grabbed the end of the cable she had released and attached it to the rod now sticking out of the ground. After testing it, she gave him a nod.

"Up, down, start, stop, and release…," he repeated.

"Emergency release," she corrected.

"I'll see you in a few," Ash said, walking backwards and releasing the cable.

Kella followed him, amazed at how easy he made descending look. He had released a long section of the cable and allowed it to hang downward. Once he walked backwards off the cliff, he glanced down, then jumped outward, sliding his hands down the cable.

She watched nervously as he worked his way down and over to the capsule. There was a large boulder on top of it. He tried to move it by pushing, but it was just too heavy. She watched him step back for several minutes, study it, pull out the laser pistol, and aim it at the boulder.

The process was slow, but he was able to blast off enough to push the rest from the capsule. He was in the process of pushing the last section off when she felt the ground rumble beneath her feet. She turned, her eyes widening in horror when she saw the wave of water in the distance rushing toward her.

"Ash! Flash flood. You have to get out of there," she ordered.

"I'm almost done," he said.

"It's too late," she whispered, staring at the rushing wall.

"Get out of there, Kella," Ash ordered.

Kella was shaking her head in denial, even though she knew that Ash couldn't see her. This wave was too wide to outrun. Glancing down, she knew there was only one way that either of them would survive.

"It is too wide, I can't outrun it. I'm coming over the side. Keep the cable taunt," she said.

"Shit!" Ash's harsh curse echoed in her ear.

"That is a distinct possibility," she replied.

It took a second for her meaning to register. It took an additional one for him to realize that she had made a joke when they were both facing almost certain death. His strained chuckle gave her the strength to lay down on the edge and wrap her feet around the cable. It grew taut under her hands and she knew that he was pulling on the other end. Crossing her feet, she allowed the weight of her body to pull her down. She gasped when she felt his hands around her waist.

"We have to get under the ledge," she said, pulling on his arm.

Ash shook his head. "I have to get Mei out. That is her pod," he said.

"You don't have time!" Kella argued, glancing up when small rocks began to rain down on them.

Ash pushed her back under the overhang and turned toward the emergency pod. "I have to," he replied with a grim expression.

Kella realized he wouldn't change his mind. She watched him, willing him to hurry. The likelihood of his friend still being alive was remote. He told her that the oxygen was depleted in his own pod and it opened. If this pod's oxygen was also depleted, there would have been no way for it to open with the size of the boulder on top of it. Whoever this Mei was, he or she would have suffocated. She bit back a growl of frustration when she felt the cliff behind her begin to vibrate violently.

"Ash, you are out of time," Kella yelled.

Ash swiped a hand across the top, clearing the glass so he could look inside. His head jerked back in horror and he glanced over at her, then looked up. Kella reached for the tether, pulling on it at the same time as Ash rose up on the emergency pod and jumped toward her. A wall of water and debris blocked her view of him. The tether in her hands grew slack before it tightened, almost pulling her out from the protective covering. Tugging on the line, she held her breath, listening for Ash's breathing.

She jerked back when a large shape suddenly flashed in front of her. A hoarse cry escaped her when a pair of strong arms wrapped around her and she was pushed back against the slick rock. She wrapped her arms around Ash's waist, holding him to her, crying, and cursing at the same time.

"Damn, but I hate this world," Ash muttered.

"I'm so sorry, Ash. There was no way, even if your friend could have escaped the pod… few know how to survive here," Kella murmured, wishing she could touch him.

"She wasn't in the pod," he said, glancing over his shoulder at the wall of water.

"But... I saw a body in it. Your face...," she said in confusion.

Ash turned back to gaze down at her. "There was a man's body in the pod. I don't know who it was. From the decomposition of the body, he must have been in it for a while," he said.

"Then, where is your friend?" she asked.

Ash shook his head. "I don't know... I don't know," he murmured, holding her close.

Chapter 26

Tallei motioned for the men to place the capsule in the center of the room. When they backed away, she walked around it, studying the markings on the outside. She motioned for one of the men to open the pod.

"Where are the contents?" she demanded, glancing at the empty interior.

One of the men nervously shifted and glanced at the other man. "It was empty. We brought it here just like we found it," he swore.

Tallei scanned the interior. It looked as if it was stripped of everything useful. If the two men were telling her the truth, then whoever had been inside the pod was still alive… and on Turbinta.

She waved her hand for the man to close the lid. Staring thoughtfully out of the window, a smile curved her lips. She would receive the credits owed to her one way or another.

"Wherever you found the capsule, there will be a stranger to this world nearby. Find this alien and I will double the credits," she ordered.

The man who spoke before cleared his throat and shot his friend another nervous look. "What does this alien look like?" the man asked.

Tallei turned to look at both men. "Different from any you have seen before. I don't know what the creature looks like. Find him. If you fail, I will kill you both. Now go!" she ordered.

"Yes, Tallei," the man mumbled, bowing and jerking his head to the other man to move.

Tallei waited until the men left her bar. She walked over to the container and ran her hand along the top. Her fingernails tapped on the glass, which loudly echoed in the deserted bar.

"Come to me, my pupil. Come. It is time to learn what happens when you disobey your mentor," Tallei murmured.

* * *

General Coleridge Landais looked around the area with revulsion. He lifted his hand to signal the guards with him. Two squadrons moved down the platform and out into the rain.

"You are sure the signal was traced here?" Coleridge asked.

Commander Taug nodded. "Yes, sir," he replied.

"Find it," Coleridge ordered.

Commander Taug bowed his head and shouted an order for the men to spread out. Coleridge gazed out over the dark, gloomy gray forest. His lips curled in distaste when the wind shifted and rain dampened his boots. There were two signals during their approach, but one disappeared.

He turned up the collar of the thick coat he wore. The remaining signal was weak. It was possible they could lose it as well. He returned to the interior of the large transport.

Nearly two hours later, he looked up from the report he was reading. Commander Taug stood at attention. Thick, gray mud covered most of the man's uniform.

"Well?" Coleridge asked.

"We found evidence of where the container landed, sir. There was a large section of material still tangled in the trees and a deep depression in the ground under it," Commander Taug said.

Coleridge rose from his chair. "I said to find the pod, not evidence of where it may have landed," he snapped.

Commander Taug bowed his head. "Yes, sir. I have my men searching the area," he stated, turning when the sound of footsteps behind him stopped.

"Sir, two men were apprehended near the vicinity of our search," the soldier stated, saluting.

Coleridge stepped out from around the desk. "Bring them to me," he ordered.

"Yes, sir," the soldier stated.

Coleridge paused by Commander Taug. The man nervously swallowed, but remained at attention. Slapping his gloves against his hand, he watched Taug wince.

"Commander, I want the pod and I want the contents, do I make myself clear?" Coleridge asked.

"I won't stop until they are both in your possession, General Landais," Taug vowed.

"See that you don't," Coleridge stated, stepping past the Commander.

* * *

Ash gripped Kella's hand as they walked back up the platform of the freighter. He was still reeling in disbelief. Mei had been in Pod One, so how was it possible that a strange alien male ended up inside? More importantly, where was Mei and was she still alive?

Kella pressed the button to close the back platform and removed her helmet. She shivered as a brisk draft of icy air blew in through the gap before it closed all the way. The journey back up the cliff and to the freighter had been exhausting.

Ash pulled his helmet off, pulled a towel out of the storage cabinet, and used it to dry the helmet before placing it in inside. Next, he removed his gloves and the thick boots. He shivered when his sock clad feet touched the cold steel floor. It didn't help that the water dripping from his suit made a small puddle around him.

"Damn, it's cold," he muttered, stripping out of the suit.

Kella nodded. "I will adjust the environmental control system," she said, trying to keep her teeth from chattering.

"You do that and I'll make something hot to eat and drink. We need to go over what we know and where the other signal was coming from," he said, taking her suit from her and hanging it up.

"I'll meet you in the galley," she replied with a nod.

Ten minutes later, the environmental system was adjusted and they were both sitting comfortably in the galley. They were studying a three-dimensional map of Turbinta. She lifted the hot cup of soup to her lips and sipped. Ash lifted his hand to tuck a strand of her hair behind her ear.

"Have I told you that I love you?" he asked, trailing his fingers across her cheek before withdrawing them to pick up his cup of soup.

Kella looked at him with a startled expression before she bowed her head. He could still see her face, thanks to having moved her hair. There was a small, pleased smile on her lips.

"I think you might have said it four times," she murmured.

He chuckled. "Have you been counting?" he asked with a raised eyebrow.

Kella glanced at him before looking away. "Yes," she murmured.

She ran her finger around the rim of her cup. His hand lifted again, this time so he could tenderly turn her head until she was looking at him. The look of uncertainty was back in her eyes.

"What is it?" he asked.

"I'm afraid to tell you that I love you," she admitted.

Ash blinked in surprise. "Why? I'm not opposed to you saying it. 'I love you, Ash' has a pretty good ring to it, don't you think? It is really easy to say, too. Four words," he teased.

She shook her head and smiled. "Tallei… Everything I have ever cared about she has taken away." Kella raised a hand and wiped at the tears that suddenly welled in her eyes and began a path down her cheek. "I even hid my box of treasures, but she found it and took it."

Ash's mouth tightened before he relaxed. "Then I'll buy you a new box and we'll find treasures together to put into it," he vowed.

Kella swallowed and pulled her chin out of his hand. "I told her once that I cared for her," she said in a defensive tone.

"Who? Tallei? And she still acted like a bitch?" Ash asked.

Kella glanced at him before gazing back down at her soup. "She took me outside and beat me. She told me that anything I cared about would be taken away from me. What if… What if it's true? What if… you are taken away from me?" she whispered.

Ash reached over and grasped Kella's hands. He turned her around until she was facing him. She reluctantly lifted her head so he could see her face. Tears dampened her cheeks and her dark eyes were almost black with fear.

"We never know when our time will come, Kella. Life is for the living. I will fight for every second of every day to be able to spend it with you. If my life ends tomorrow, I want to know I have no regrets. Loving you… You are the most beautiful person I've ever seen. We can't live our lives in fear. Tallei uses fear to control you. Now you have to make a decision. You can let fear control you or you can control it. You are the only one who has the power to make that decision, Kella. I can't make it for you and Tallei can't force it on you," Ash said.

Kella's fingers tightened around his hands. He could see the internal battle that was raging inside her. He could also see the moment she triumphed.

"I love you, Ashton Haze," she breathed. "I love you," she said again, the smile growing on her lips.

Ash laughed and pulled her into his arms. "Twice more and we'll be even," he chuckled.

"I love you," she said, leaning back to cup his face before capturing his lips.

The sound of a ping finally penetrated their consciousness. They reluctantly pulled apart. Ash frowned and glanced around.

"What is that?" he asked.

Kella paled and a shiver ran through her body as she pulled away from him. She glanced out of the doorway before turning to look at him. He didn't miss the slight tremble to her hand when she brushed her hair behind her ear.

"It is Tallei," she answered.

Chapter 27

"Do not let her see you," Kella warned, motioning for him to sit down in the copilot seat.

Ash's lips tightened, but he didn't say anything. Kella glanced at him before schooling her face into an unemotional mask. Once she was ready, she leaned forward and activated the communications console.

"Tallei," she greeted.

Tallei was silent for several seconds. Ash recognized it for what it was – a power play. He sat back in his seat and rolled his eyes. As far as he was concerned, two could play that game. Obviously, Kella and he were both on the same page.

"Your time is up," Tallei finally replied.

Kella shook her head. "I have two days left," she replied.

"Not any longer," Tallei stated.

"The contract stated the time period. I have two days left," Kella insisted.

Tallei was silent for a moment before she spoke again. "Bring the alien to me, Kella, and I will not kill you."

"No," Kella replied.

Tallei's lips tightened into a straight line. "The Legion forces are here. Bring the alien to me. I order you to obey," she hissed.

"No, Tallei. I will not bring him to you," Kella said in a quiet voice. "I no longer answer to you."

Tallei's lip curled in disgust. "Do you think you love him, Kella? Do you wish to collect him and place him in a box with your other treasures?" she asked in a mocking tone.

"Damn! I say daammmn, but how do you spell bitch?" Ash asked rhetorically, finally having had enough. He stood up and stepped behind Kella. He placed his hands on her shoulders and squeezed them in support. "You know, they have places for psychopaths like you."

Tallei looked him up and down, or at least as much as she could. If that look was supposed to frighten or intimidate him, Ash could have told the bitch she was wasting her time. He had never been one to take anyone's opinion personal.

"You are arrogant," Tallei stated.

"Yep, to the bone," Ash agreed with an insulting smirk.

"You are reckless," Tallei observed.

"And handsome, witty, charming, and a host of other adjectives. I'll send you a dictionary if you need help with the definitions," Ash replied sarcastically.

Tallei's eyes flashed at his insulting tone. "You will come to regret your disdain of a Master Turbinta, alien."

Ash leaned forward, staring down Tallei's one good eye. "Not likely, bitch. Kella is no longer under your thumb. If you come near her again, you'll have to deal with us both," he promised.

"Oh, I will deal with her – and with you, when you come to me. You'll come quickly if you wish to rescue the other one of your kind," Tallei said, stepping to the side so the room was in view.

Kella's loud hiss echoed through the cockpit. Ash's hands tightened on her shoulders. His eyes narrowed on the emergency pod in the center of the dim room. On the side, he could see the large number five with a circle around it – Sergi.

"You know where to come, Kella. You have one hour or I will use the alien I found inside to show you what happens to those who displease me," Tallei stated before the transmission ended.

"Son-of-a-bitch!" Ash cursed, lifting his hands to run through his hair. He turned and pointed at the screen. "I'm going to kill her sorry ass."

"Ash…," Kella said, rising out of her seat and placing her hand on his arm. "Tallei… she is very dangerous. She will do what she says."

"How does she know where we are?" he suddenly asked, turning to look at her. "She said to be there in an hour. How does she know that we can be?"

Kella paled and swayed. Ash gripped her arms to steady her. He bent and looked in her eyes urgently.

"There must be another tracking device. I found one and destroyed it. I… She must have hidden a second on the ship," Kella said.

"We don't have time to look for it, but now that we know, we use it to our advantage," Ash bit out.

"What do you mean?" Kella asked in confusion.

Ash glanced around before turning back to look at her. "Tallei knows how to fight like a Turbinta, right?" he asked.

Kella paused for a moment, then her eyes widened as she took in his meaning. "But not like a human!" she exclaimed. "What are we going to do?"

"Good old fashion guerrilla warfare darling – Ashton Haze style," he chuckled.

..*

Coleridge wiped the blood off of his hands and stepped over the body of the second man he just killed. He ignored the rain soaking his coat. It was a small price to pay for the information he obtained.

"That, Commander Taug, is how you locate the information you need," he stated, walking past the dead body.

"Yes, sir," Taug replied.

"We leave immediately for the town," Coleridge ordered.

Commander Taug whipped the water from his face with a trembling hand. "Yes, sir. What should we do once we have the container?" he asked.

Coleridge paused and turned to look at Taug. "On second thought, you will remain here to continue the search for the contents that are still missing, Commander. I will retrieve the container myself," he replied.

"S... Sir? Without a transport? What about my men?" Commander Taug asked, taking a step forward.

Coleridge waved a hand toward six shivering men standing behind Taug. "You can keep them with you," he said, turning to continue up the platform.

"Sir! Without proper supplies, we'll freeze to death out here," Taug protested.

Coleridge stepped into the transport and turned to look down the platform dispassionately at Taug. "Then I suggest you decide which man is going to give you his uniform to help keep you warm," he replied before nodding for the platform to be raised.

"Send a message to the First Officer informing him he has just been promoted to Commander. Also inform him that I want a squadron of fighters on standby. I want the city leveled once the container is retrieved and we have departed," Coleridge ordered.

"Yes, sir," the soldier standing next to him replied with a salute.

Coleridge walked to his office. He could feel the rumble of the transport as it lifted off. Shrugging out of his damp coat, he tossed it over one of the chairs. Walking around the desk, he opened a panel, drew out another coat, and pulled it on. After he finished fastening it, he reached inside again and pulled out several weapons – including the Knight of the Gallant Staff he was given many, many years ago by his mentor – Jemar de Rola.

A wave of resentment washed through him. Jemar must have sensed Coleridge's desire for more. His mentor presented him with a Staff, but withheld the knowledge of how to create one or to pass the Staff on to another.

Coleridge ran his fingers over the intricate design. He was unwilling to risk destroying the Staff. The countless Staffs he confiscated and ordered re-engineered had ended in disaster. This one belonged to him. No one – not Roan, not even Andri – would ever be able to use it against him.

"Sir," the soldier he sent with the message stood in the doorway.

Coleridge closed the panel and turned. "Yes," he acknowledged.

"We will be landing in the city in a few minutes," the soldier informed him.

"Perfect," Coleridge replied.

..*

Ash held up his hand. Kella nodded and pointed. The image of the map Kella drew flashed through his mind. The bar was at the far end of the compact city. There were two entrances, one in the front and one in the back.

Kella thought he was crazy when he first came up with his plan. After some rationalizing and a tiny bit of begging for her to trust him, she finally agreed that it would be the last thing Tallei would expect.

They auto-programmed the freighter to arrive in ten minutes just outside the city where a landing pad was available for traders willing to risk dealing with the Turbinta for the chance of a large profit. Kella programmed the freighter to return to her own landing pad.

Ash always said that strange things happened for a reason. The Legion shuttle, while not in the best of shape on the outside, was just the ticket to get them here early. For once, Ash was thankful Kella had been overly-productive when she was scared to talk to him. The plan was simple – he would walk in the front door of the bar while Kella walked in the back. If the bitch gave him any lip, he'd knock her ass out – with the nice little darts that Josh so generously left behind for him.

While he would love to kill the old hag, it still went against every code of honor in him to kill a woman – even one as bad as Tallei. He was surprised at Kella's response to that. She had vehemently argued that Tallei should not be left alive.

"The freighter will land in ten minutes," she murmured in the comlink he had in his ear.

"I'm walking down the street," he said, stepping out from around the building.

"Remember, do not speak, and ignore anyone who might bump into you," she warned. "Oh, and make sure they don't take anything if they do."

"Damn, I feel like I'm back in Vegas," he chuckled.

"Ash," Kella groaned.

"I know. No talking, keep the pickpockets away," he murmured. "I love you, Kella."

The loud sigh in his ear made him grin. "You are making me crazy," she hissed.

"Tell me or I'll start crooning Singing in the Rain," he teased.

"I love you, Ashton Haze. Please don't get yourself killed," Kella whispered in his ear.

The smile on Ash's face faded. "The same goes for you, sweetheart. I'd better go silent. I've got someone giving me a weird look. I don't want him thinking I'm talking to him. Never mind, he is a she," he murmured.

"Be careful," she whispered before going silent.

Ash glanced over his shoulder at the cloaked figure he just passed. He couldn't see the woman's face, just the edge of her skirt peaking below her cloak. Her slow movement didn't cause him any concern, especially since she turned down the street.

He glanced around, keeping his head down as much as he could and still see. There weren't many people about. If this was a city, it was surely one of the smallest ones he had ever seen. It looked more like a medieval village straight from a horror movie.

He paused outside of Tallei's bar. It had no name. He pushed the door open, stepped inside, and shut the door behind him. From the lack of customers, he decided marketing wasn't Tallei's talent. He glanced at the emergency pod sitting in the center of the room, but walked past it like it was normal to have one sitting in the middle of a bar. He walked over and sat down in a chair near the front window, making sure he had the wall to his back. A moment later, the door opened and several more people entered. Ash's gaze narrowed when he saw the stooped woman from the street enter last. She was carrying a basket now.

Ash immediately recognized Tallei when she stepped from the back of the bar. She spoke in a low, menacing tone to the men who had entered. One of the men started to protest, but the other two men with him grabbed him by the arm and pulled him toward the door.

"Nebi mau keti mi," Tallei ordered, waving her hand at the men.

Ash watched the men stumble back out into the rain. He remained seated in the shadows. She sneered and shut the door, locking it with a large key. Turning, she paused when she saw him sitting in the corner.

"Nebi mau keti mi!" Tallei snarled.

Ash leaned forward and pulled the hood off of his head. He tilted his head and grinned. He really wished he had a camera because her face was the perfect Kodak moment.

"Sorry, bitch, I don't understand what you're saying, but I have to say, if your tone is anything to go by, you need some serious counseling on how to run a business ," Ash observed.

"You!" Tallei snarled.

Ash shook his head and tsked. "I guess I really should introduce myself seeing as how we are going to be related and all. The name is Ashton Haze. Lt. Commander Ashton Haze, United States Navy," he introduced himself, standing slowly.

"I could not care less what you are called. Where is Kella?" Tallei demanded.

"I am here, Tallei," Kella said from behind her mentor.

Tallei turned and stepped back, her good eye narrowed on the laser pistol Kella aimed at her. Ash cleared his throat when Tallei's hand moved down along her side.

"I wouldn't, lady. I promised myself I'd never kill a woman if I could help it. Please don't make me break that promise," he warned, stepping out from behind the table.

Tallei's gaze moved down to his hand resting on his Staff. Her fingers curled and she looked back up at him. Ash didn't miss the subtle expression of disbelief in her eye.

"The legend is true? The Ancient Knights of the Gallant Order have returned?" Tallei asked with a sneer.

"Let's just say we're here and you have someone I want. Where is he?" Ash demanded.

"He… The one who was in the container?" Tallei asked, glancing at the empty pod.

"Yeah, that one," Ash said.

Tallei turned to look at Kella. "I will tell you where he is in return for payment," she replied with a shrug.

"No," Kella said, her voice strong and her aim steady even as her stomach churned with fear. "You will tell us where he is now, Tallei. If you do, I might let you live."

"Payment?" Ash asked, warily watching Tallei walk closer to the pod. He moved so he could see her hands. "What kind of payment?"

"I want Kella," Tallei said, stopping in front of the pod.

"Fuck that," Ash replied, his gaze flickering to the stony mask on Kella's face when Tallei said her name. It was obvious that Kella had suspected what her mentor would demand. "Kella is not an option."

Tallei turned and smiled. "I expected you to refuse," she said.

Ash heard the sound of something dropping to the floor at the same time as Tallei finished her last word. He caught a brief glance of a red light a moment before Tallei kicked it toward him. A low curse escaped Ash and he dove to the side.

A loud explosion tossed the nearest table and chair up into the air. Tallei turned at the same time as Kella fired. Ash covered his ringing ears and shook his head. He couldn't see Kella from this angle. All he could see were the legs of the tables and chairs and bottom of the pod.

He rose up and stumbled back away from the blade that came close to slicing his neck wide open. He jumped back again when Tallei attacked him with a second blade. In the background, he could see the old woman kneeling over Kella's prone form. A low hiss of pain escaped him when the tip of the knife cut through the sleeve of his robe.

"Kella!" Ash yelled, glancing between her and Tallei.

"She lies dying by my blade, Ancient Knight," Tallei sneered. "I told her what would happen if she betrayed me."

Ash drew in a deep breath and stepped back. "She loved you," he said, moving into a defensive stance.

"And it made her weak! She should have killed me while my back was turned. Her affection for me left her vulnerable to my blade," Tallei replied.

"You are one sick bitch," Ash said, blocking her attack.

"I am the only family she has," Tallei replied, stepping to the side when Ash blocked another of her blows.

"Family? You call beating her, using her, and training her to kill being a family?" Ash demanded.

Tallei's cackle really grated on his nerves. There was a note of insanity to it. This woman really wasn't working on all eight cylinders.

"I was taken as a child and trained just as I took Kella. I was older than Kella was, but I learned fast." Tallei palmed a knife strapped to her arm and threw it. She hissed when it missed, striking the wall behind Ash when he twisted at the last minute. She snarled and continued to talk, hoping to distract Ash using his feelings for Kella against him.

"I remembered my true family. The one that did nothing to come for me. After my first mission, I returned to the world I remembered and I found them. My younger sister, who was just a babe when I left, had grown up. She had joined with a man and had a daughter. A daughter who should have been mine. A family that should have been mine – but they did not care enough to fight for me," Tallei sneered.

She threw another knife. She missed him again when he ducked. He was trying to use her blindness against her. Fury coursed through her. This time, she pulled two of the knives from one of the belts at her waist.

Ash blocked Tallei when she lashed out at him. He grabbed her wrist and twisted. The knife in her hand fell to the floor. He blocked the knife in her other hand when she brought it up to stab him in the stomach. She jumped back.

"She is your niece?" Ash asked in disbelief.

"What did you do to my parents?" Kella asked in a trembling voice.

Tallei jerked around in surprise. Her gaze flew from Kella's pale face to the unusual man with white-blonde hair standing next to her. She turned back to look at Ash. Deep down, Ash was hoping Tallei would get a major case of whiplash from the way she had to turn her head to see them all with just one eye.

"Hey, Sergi. Long time, man," Ash quipped, trying not to reveal his own surprise.

"Привет. Hi, Ash," Sergi replied with a grin.

"How long were you planning on just watching?" Ash demanded.

Sergi shrugged. "I don't know. When you greet a woman by calling her a bitch, I figure it is probably a personal disagreement and I should stay out of it," he replied.

"Kella, you okay, love?" Ash asked, seeing the blood coating her shoulder.

Kella nodded, not taking her eyes off of Tallei. "What did you do to my parents?" she asked again in a quiet voice.

Tallei's lip curled. "I killed them. Your father was the first to die, then your mother. I left her alive long enough to see me take you. She knew what your life would be," she said.

Kella swayed. Memories flashed through her mind in a kaleidoscope of horrifying images. Her mother's weeping. Her father's sightless eyes and his body lying in a pool of blood. Her screams as she tried to hold on to her mother.

"I remember…," she whispered.

"Sergi, catch her," Ash ordered at the same time as Sergi's arm wrapped around Kella's waist.

Using the tip of his boot, Ash picked up the Staff Kubo gave him and extended it. His eyes glittered with fury, but he didn't let it distract him. Tallei's hand went to the belt at her waist and she pulled it off with a loud snap.

Ash saw the line of razor sharp blades expand out of the whip that formed. His fingers pressed on the Staff and twin, glowing orbs appeared at each end. Tallei snapped the whip at him. Ash twirled the Staff in both directions with lightning speed. Sections of the whip skidded across the floor, severed by the power locked into the ends of the Staff.

Tallei threw the remains of the whip at him and started to reach into her robe when she staggered to the side. Her good eye widened before it grew dim and she fell forward. Ash jerked back in surprise and looked over at Sergi and Kella.

Sergi pointed at Kella. "She did it," he said.

Kella stood still, Sergi's arm still supporting her. Her arm was stretched out and the laser pistol raised. Sergi scooped her up when her legs gave out from under her and her hand lowered as the adrenaline that was fueling her suddenly drained away.

"Kella."

Ash stepped over Tallei. He briefly glanced down at the dark mark in the center of the old woman's back. It was better than she deserved for all the misery she had put Kella though. Stepping around the pod, he hurried over to Sergi.

"She is in shock," Sergi said.

Ash nodded, taking Kella out of Sergi's arms. He glanced around for a place to set her down so he could examine her wound better. The only place was the pod.

"It looks like we are about to have company, Ash. We need to leave," Sergi said with a nod of his head toward the front window.

Ash cursed when he saw a group of Legion soldiers marching down the center of the road. In front was a man who suspiciously resembled General Dracula Landais. He wondered if they were related.

"The cellar," Kella said. "There is a tunnel that leads to the spaceport. It comes up under my freighter."

"Go. I will be there in a moment," Sergi replied.

Ash nodded and turned. He shifted Kella in his arms and growled for her to be quiet when she insisted he put her down. He finally relented when they reached the bottom of the stairs, but only because it was too narrow to carry her through.

"Where's Sergi?" Ash snapped, waiting in the hidden doorway inside an empty barrel of liquor.

"No worries. I thought we might need some refreshments to celebrate finding each other," Sergi said, crossing from the bottom of the stairs and holding up two bottles of liquor.

"You are crazier than I am!" Ash muttered, nodding for Sergi to follow Kella.

"You are just now figuring that out? Do you know if anyone else made it?" Sergi asked.

Ash nodded. "Josh did," he said.

Sergi paused and looked back at Ash. "What of Mei and Julia?" he asked in a quiet voice.

"We don't know," Ash admitted. "I'll tell you once we are out of this place."

Sergi nodded. "I hope there are better planets than this one. It reminds me too much of home," he complained.

Ash glanced ahead at Kella. She walked at a steady pace, her back straight and stiff, but he didn't miss the fact that she occasionally raised her hand to brush it across her face. His heart ached for her.

"I love you," he murmured softly, knowing she would be able to hear him in the comlink.

Her head bowed and her shoulders trembled, but she didn't slow down. "I love you, too, Ashton Haze –

Epilogue

General Coleridge Landais stood in the center of the bar. In one corner, the shattered remains of a table and chair littered the floor. He turned when one of the soldiers found blood on the floor. It was obvious there had been a fight, but that was not unusual for such an establishment.

He turned his gaze back to the pod sitting in the center of the room. It was the one that was missing from the forest. Leaves and mud still coated the bottom of it.

"Open it," he ordered, stepping to the side.

Two of the soldiers stepped forward. It took them a moment to find the release. The lid slowly opened, revealing the covered form inside. Coleridge frowned. The cloak had mud along the edges of it. He snapped his fingers and motioned to the soldier near the end of the pod to remove the covering. Fury poured through him when he saw the blank eyes staring up at him. One eye was cloudy.

Curling his fingers into a fist. He bit back the loud curse that threatened to escape him. Instead, he turned to the soldier from the transport.

"What is your name?" Coleridge demanded.

"Sergeant Ri Manta, sir," Manta replied.

"Commander Manta, discard the body, have this pod delivered to the Battle Cruiser, and order the destruction of the city, including any ships leaving the spaceport," Coleridge ordered.

"Yes, sir," Manta replied, turning to bark out orders to several of the soldiers.

Coleridge walked over to the window and stared out. They were in possession of two capsules. He knew of at least two survivors, possibly a third. One of the capsules that landed here had disappeared. He doubted it would ever be found. That did not mean that whoever had been inside it did not survive as well. Finally, there was one more – the one Roan was retrieving.

"Sir, the transport is ready for pick up," Manta stated.

Coleridge lifted his hand to let the man know he heard him. Turning away, he scanned the room. In the back corner on a table was a basket. Walking over to it, he glanced down inside it. His lips tightened when he saw a small patch inside. Lifting it up, he held it up to the light. It had the same pattern as the one from Torrian and from Tesla Terra.

"Let's go," he snapped, turning and striding out of the bar.

The emblem and the strange configuration of stars taunted him. What did they mean? There was one person who knew the legend better than anyone. The archives on Jeslean were destroyed, along with the scholars there, but there was one who still lived. It was time to pay a visit to the old man who lived the life of a hermit.

* * *

"She's real quiet," Sergi said.

Ash nodded. "She's been through a lot," he replied. "Thanks for staying with her and doctoring her up."

"You teach me how to fly one of these, and I'll be happy to take over," Sergi said. "I'll go sit up front. If I see any bad guys, I'll play with some of the weapons your girlfriend has loaded on this thing."

Ash absently nodded. "Just don't blow anything up!" he called out as an afterthought.

He chuckled when Sergi went off on a tangent in Russian. Sergi was trying not to show how upset he was when he found out that Mei was not in her capsule and they knew nothing about Julia. He shared how he woke up in the forest on Turbinta. At first, he thought he was transported back home. Sergi had actually been very happy when he discovered he wasn't back in Russia.

"I made some soup for you," Kella murmured.

Ash looked up in surprise to see Kella standing in front of him. He reached for the cup and wrapped his arm around her waist. Together, they walked back over to the table and slid down onto the bench seat.

"How are you feeling?" Ash asked, placing the cup of soup on the table.

Kella shrugged. "I heal fast," she replied.

Ash lifted his hand and tilted her chin back so she was forced to look at him. "That's not what I meant," he said.

Kella gave him a watery smile. "Sad," she admitted.

Ash brushed her lips in a tender kiss before he pulled her close. "You are allowed to be," he said.

Kella chuckled and snuggled up against him. "What do I do now? The only thing I've ever known is how to be an assassin," she murmured.

Ash picked up his cup and took a sip. He thought about it for several minutes before he released a chuckle. Hell, life was crazy; why not make it completely nuts?

"Well, I heard about this really cool rebellion against some major asswipes. Then there's this Ancient dude who doesn't know shit about this alien world he woke up in, but everyone thinks he and his friends are these superheroes or something. And well…."

"I think one of them especially needs extra protection," she said, sitting up and smiling at him.

"He needs a bodyguard, someone who can be with him 24/7 or whatever the cycles are here," Ash said, setting his cup back down on the table again and turning toward her.

"I accept," Kella murmured, lifting a hand to cup his cheek.

"She'll have to teach him new words and how to fly a freighter, but she'll have to be willing to work for cheap," he said, turning his head to press a kiss against her palm.

"I understand she accepts lessons in self-defense as payment," Kella replied.

"Most of all, she'll have to love me," Ash finished.

Kella smiled. "Only if he tells her every morning that she is the most beautiful woman he has ever seen," she whispered, leaning forward to meet his lips.

Neither one of them heard Sergi stop and glance into the galley. Turning, he retraced his steps back to the cockpit. There would be plenty of time to ask questions about the weapons systems.

"Oh Mei, you would be loving this," Sergi said with a sad grin. "To Julia and Mei. May you both find a place in this new world."

Sergi lifted the stolen bottle of liquor to his lips. There was a lot to learn about this new world, but he wasn't alone anymore. He just might survive longer than expected.

To be continued:

Survival Skills: Project Gliese 581g

Sergi wakes to discover that the wars he left behind on Earth were just a training ground for what is to come. He and his friends are caught in the middle of a new war and he will need to use all of his skills to survive.

Additional Books and Information

If you loved this story by me (S.E. Smith) please leave a review. You can also take a look at additional books and sign up for my newsletter at http://sesmithfl.com and http://sesmithya.com to hear about my latest releases or keep in touch using the following links:

http://sesmithfl.com
http://sesmithfl.com/?s=newsletter
https://www.facebook.com/se.smith.5
https://twitter.com/sesmithfl
http://www.pinterest.com/sesmithfl/
http://sesmithfl.com/blog/
http://www.sesmithromance.com/forum/

Excerpts of S.E. Smith Books

If you would like to read more S.E. Smith stories, she recommends Touch of Frost, the first in her Magic, New Mexico series. Or if you prefer a Paranormal or Western with a twist, you can check out Lily's Cowboys or Indiana Wild…

Additional Books by S.E. Smith

Short Stories and Novellas

Dragon Lords of Valdier Novella
For the Love of Tia (Book 4.1)

Dragonlings of Valdier Novellas
A Dragonling's Easter (Book 1.1)
A Dragonling's Haunted Halloween (Book 1.2)
Night of the Demented Symbiots (Halloween 2)

A Dragonling's Magical Christmas (Book 1.3)
The Dragonlings' Very Special Valentine (Book 1.4)

Pets in Space Anthology
A Mate for Matrix

Marastin Dow Warriors Short Story
A Warrior's Heart (Book 1.1)

Lords of Kassis Novella
Rescuing Mattie (Book 3.1)

The Fairy Tale Novella
The Beast Prince
*Free Audiobook of The Beast Prince is available:
https://soundcloud.com/sesmithfl/sets/the-beast-prince-the-fairy-tale-series

Boxsets / Bundles

Dragon Lords of Valdier Boxset Books 1-3
The Alliance Boxset Books 1-3

Science Fiction Romance / Paranormal Novels

Cosmos' Gateway Series
Tink's Neverland (Book 1)
Hannah's Warrior (Book 2)
Tansy's Titan (Book 3)
Cosmos' Promise (Book 4)
Merrick's Maiden (Book 5)

Curizan Warrior Series
Ha'ven's Song (Book 1)

Gracie's Touch (Book 1)
Krac's Firebrand (Book 2)

Paranormal / Time Travel Romance Novels

Spirit Pass Series
Indiana Wild (Book 1)
Spirit Warrior (Book 2)

Second Chance Series
Lily's Cowboys (Book 1)
Touching Rune (Book 2)

Paranormal Novels

More Than Human Series
Ella and the Beast (Book 1)

Science Fiction / Action Adventure Novels

Project Gliese 581G Series
Command Decision (Book 1)
First Awakenings (Book 2)

Young Adult Novels

Breaking Free Series
Voyage of the Defiance (Book 1)
Capture of the Defiance (Book 2)

The Dust Series
Dust: Before and After (Book 1)

Recommended Reading Order Lists:

http://sesmithfl.com/reading-list-by-events/
http://sesmithfl.com/reading-list-by-series/

About the Author

S.E. Smith is a ***New York Times, USA TODAY, International, and Award-Winning*** Bestselling author of science fiction, romance, fantasy, paranormal, and contemporary works for adults, young adults, and children. She enjoys writing a wide variety of genres that pull her readers into worlds that take them away.

CPSIA information can be obtained
at www.ICGtesting.com
Printed in the USA
LVOW10s1053030417
529424LV00009B/20/P